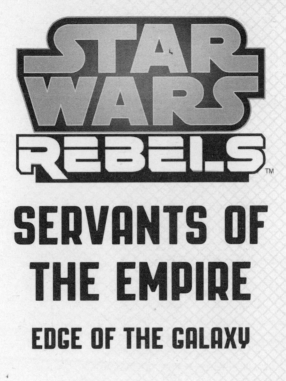

SERVANTS OF THE EMPIRE

EDGE OF THE GALAXY

BY JASON FRY

EGMONT

We bring stories to life

First published in Great Britain 2014
by Egmont UK Limited, The Yellow Building,
1 Nicholas Road, London W11 4AN.

Cover illustration by John-Paul Balmet

ISBN 978 1 4052 7581 1
59263/1
Printed in UK

Stay safe online. Any website addresses listed in this book are correct at the
time of going to print. However, Egmont is not responsible for content hosted by
third parties. Please be aware that online content can be subject to change
and websites can contain content that is unsuitable for children.
We advise that all children are supervised
when using the internet.

For Doug and Erik, with whom
the wonders of the Tomb of Horrors and
the Temples of Syrinx were explored.
—J. F.

PROLOGUE:
SUMMER

After the first hour of the party Zare Leonis stopped pretending to look happy. It was a beautiful evening on Lothal. All around the top deck of his family's apartment the lights of Capital City glittered and blinked, and he could smell the faint sweetness of seedpods and blossoms, carried on a gentle breeze from the grasslands beyond the city.

Besides their neighbours, the guests included scientists who worked with Zare's parents at the Ministry of Agriculture, ministers from a variety of Imperial departments, and a scattering of officers in crisp olive-grey uniforms. Zare didn't know most of the guests, but they knew who he was; people kept stopping to shake his hand.

But the congratulations weren't for him, and neither was the party. All of it was for his older sister,

Dhara – the person he wanted to talk with most, and the one who had the least time for him.

'Zare! Isn't it marvellous about your sister!' said a rail-thin woman from the Ag Ministry whom Zare vaguely remembered was an assistant under-something to a deputy somebody. He managed a half smile, mumbled an excuse, and turned away only to hear a familiar whir of servomotors and feel a pinch at his sleeve.

'Assistant Vice Minister Sarkos is a guest in this house,' said Auntie Nags, her photoreceptors an angry red. 'You are nearly fifteen years old, which means you know how to make conversation – or at least eye contact. And don't let me catch you slouching, Zare Leonis.'

Zare started to snarl a response, then hung his head. He couldn't yell at Auntie Nags. The ancient nanny droid had cared for him since he was a baby, just like she'd cared for his father, and his father, and so on back through the generations. No one remembered exactly how long she'd been in the family, or what her original model number had been. As long as there'd been Leonises, it seemed, she'd been there.

'I'm sorry, Auntie Nags,' Zare said, and the droid's photoreceptors dimmed and turned yellow. 'I just feel like I don't belong here. Dhara's going to the Imperial Academy, and I'm just some stupid useless kid in the way.'

Auntie Nags tilted her head and her eyes switched to a cool green.

'You are a Leonis, and that is the furthest thing from stupid or useless,' she said. 'You will adjust to the Junior Academy for Applied Sciences, you will earn the marks expected of a Leonis, your application to the Imperial Academy of Lothal will be accepted, and you will join Dhara next year. Until then, you must be patient.'

'I know,' Zare said. 'It's just hard, that's all.'

'Anything worth doing is hard,' Auntie Nags said, eyes flashing briefly yellow before returning to green. 'Now then, Zare, I have jogan clusters to serve. There's Ames Bunkle, and he looks lonely – his parents are on assignment and couldn't be here tonight. A good host would go talk to him.'

The old nanny droid wheeled away. Zare looked sorrowfully at his sister, who was nodding at something Minister Maketh Tua was saying. Then he turned to where Ames Bunkle was leaning on the railing, looking out into the night. A broad-shouldered boy tanned by the sun, Ames was sixteen, the same as Dhara, and also entering the Academy in a couple of weeks. His parents lived on a lower floor of their building. They were colleagues of the Leonises at the Ag Ministry – something to do with fertiliser research,

Zare thought.

'Are you excited about the Academy?' Zare asked, and Ames looked startled.

'More like scared stiff,' he said.

'What for?'

'Lots of people wash out of the Academy, you know,' Ames said. 'It's tough.'

'But so are you,' Zare said. 'It's a shame I'm getting to AppSci right after you left – your mum told me you hold the school record for carries in grav-ball.'

Ames smiled. 'Yep – set it against Forked River last season. The physical things don't scare me. It's the learning – never liked being cooped up in a classroom, and can't ever remember that stuff. Your sister will probably be governor someday, but I'll be lucky to make stormtrooper.'

'So?' Zare asked. 'You'll still get to serve the Empire. There are still parts of the Outer Rim in the hands of pirates – or worse.'

Something whined in the night. The two boys looked up and saw the faint shapes of TIE fighters on patrol. They turned to follow the fighters' path by watching the red lights on the rear of their fuselages.

'Think those were the new SFS P-s4 ion engines?' Zare asked, still scanning the night sky. 'They sounded different somehow.'

'They *were* SFS P-s4s,' said a voice that didn't belong to Ames. The accent was clipped and cultured. It was the voice of someone who came from the Core Worlds, or wanted people to think he did. 'The new engines are an improvement over the P-s3s – fuel efficiency is fifteen per cent better and the heat exchangers are less prone to flux. Which means the pitch of the ion engines is a little higher.'

The speaker was a man in his mid-twenties, with pale skin and close-cropped dark hair. He wore an Imperial military uniform.

'Lieutenant Piers Roddance,' he said. His handshake was strong, and Zare wondered if the young officer was trying to crush his hand.

'Of course,' Roddance said when Zare introduced himself. 'I look forward to watching your sister's progress at the Academy.'

'Me too,' Zare said. 'Oh, this is Ames Bunkle – he's going to the Academy, too.'

'Ah,' Roddance said, his pale blue eyes sizing up Ames's rough-hewn hands and faded formal tunic. Roddance kept his hands behind his back, Zare noticed, thinking Auntie Nags wouldn't approve of that.

'How do you know all that stuff about the P-s4s,

Lieutenant?' Zare asked quickly.

'My duties include inspecting the Sienar Fleet Systems' new facilities here on Lothal,' Roddance said. 'We just received three squadrons of the new TIEs last week. Maybe you'll fly one someday, Zare.'

'Or maybe Ames will,' Zare said.

'Nuh-uh – give me firm ground under my feet,' Ames said. 'Uh, sir . . . have you seen those new two-man walkers?'

'The AT-DPs,' Roddance said. 'Proper terminology is a rule of the Academy, Bunkle. Yes, they're remarkable machines – faster and better armoured than the old AT-RTs.'

'What about firepower?' Ames asked eagerly. 'That ball cannon looks *mean*.'

'I've seen a single shot punch through medium vehicle plating,' Roddance said. 'That mean enough for you?'

'Wizard!' Ames said.

'And having a separate gunner makes them suitable for infantry support, not just recon,' Roddance said. 'The 291st Legion used them to clear out a nest of Thalassian slavers on Galpos II, and then as the vanguard in urban fighting on Mendavi. I can assure you they were most impressive.'

'I heard about the Galpos raid!' Bunkle said. 'You

were there, sir?'

Pink spots bloomed in Roddance's cheeks.

'Well, no – but I've studied the reports extensively,' he said. 'Such displays of military strength will soon be seen everywhere in the galaxy. Our Empire is strong – and growing stronger. Nothing will drag us back into the mire of Separatism and insurgency that the Republic allowed to fester.'

Roddance looked up into the night and smiled. His eyes were bright and eager, and the look on his face made Zare feel momentarily uneasy.

'The Emperor began by offering mercy to fools who wanted to cling to the past – senators who put their own advancement over the needs of the citizenry, and greedy corporations, and pretend patriots. They took advantage of the Emperor's patience, but more and more they are learning of his wrath.'

'Just hope I get to help deliver the message,' Ames said, grinning.

'Governor Pryce is here,' Zare said, finding himself eager to change the subject. 'Mum hoped she'd come.'

The governor moved through the guests with aides on either side, smiling and shaking hands. Auntie Nags was rolling back and forth outside the knot of people waiting to talk to the governor. She had a tray of drinks balanced on one synth-flesh hand, which tipped precariously as she shied from potential collisions.

Zare's parents reached the governor, with Dhara standing between them. As their mother chatted with Governor Pryce, Dhara turned her head and looked straight at Zare. As always, she seemed to know where he was without having to search for him. A smile split her dark brown face and she gestured for him to come over – and, he could tell, to hurry.

'Excuse me, Lieutenant,' Zare said to Roddance. 'Come on, Ames! You are about to be an Academy cadet, aren't you?'

Ames nodded sheepishly and the two boys worked their way through the crowd to the Leonises. Behind Governor Pryce, Zare recognised Supplymaster Yogar Lyste, Commandant Cumberlayne Aresko, and his hulking aide, Myles Grint. Zare's father, Leo, patted Zare's head and Zare raised an arm to fend off further displays of affection.

'And this is our son, Zare,' Leo said. 'He's about to start at AppSci. Next year he'll be eligible for the Academy, too.'

'Arihnda Pryce,' the governor said, extending a slim hand. 'Your sister's told me about you, Zare. I'm very glad to welcome you and your family to Lothal, and honoured that such accomplished scientists would send not one but two children into Imperial service.'

'We've only been here a month, but Lothal already feels like home,' Leo said. 'And the honour is entirely ours, Governor.'

'Uh-oh, Dad's going to make a speech,' Zare said, and his family laughed.

'Just a short one,' Leo said, smiling. 'Tepha and I remember when our inventions were stuck in the Republic courts, and when the Trade Federation let our genetically modified crops rot in warehouses to protect their profit margins. The Empire changed all that – now our work is improving the lives of Imperial citizens, and the Trade Federation is just a bad dream. So we are honoured to have our daughter serve the Empire that has given us so much.'

Governor Pryce smiled and bowed her head.

'You should have been a politician, Leo,' she said. 'How about you do the talking and I just clap my hands and eat more of these delicious jogan clusters?'

'Oh, no, Governor,' Tepha Leonis said. 'For my husband that really was a short speech. Give him a chance and we'll be stuck listening to him all night.'

'Governor, I'd like you to meet one of my Academy classmates,' Dhara said. 'The strong, silent young man here is Ames Bunkle.'

As a flustered Ames tried not to fall over his own tongue, Dhara nudged Zare and retreated with him to the railing.

'Aren't there people you need to talk to?' Zare asked, expecting Auntie Nags to roll up and lecture him for monopolising his sister's time.

'Oh, probably,' Dhara said. 'But I wanted to talk to you, Zare. I'm going to miss you, you know.'

'Me too,' Zare said, and heard his voice catch in his throat. Embarrassed, he stared out into the dark beyond Capital City.

'But we'll get to talk regularly once orientation's over,' Dhara said. 'I'll let you know what the Academy's like so you have a head start next year.'

'Next year,' moaned Zare. 'You may as well say forever.'

Dhara smiled and squeezed his shoulder.

'I know it's a new school, but you'll find your way and make friends, like you always have,' she said. 'And you'll have Auntie Nags to make sure you study each night when you come home.'

'Oh, now everything sounds perfect,' Zare said, and his sister smiled again.

'Anyway, the time will pass before you know it,' said Dhara. 'And then your biggest problem will be trying to live up to the reputation of your beautiful, brilliant older sister.'

She elevated her chin, then grinned. Zare had to laugh.

'Looks like it's time for the governor's speech,' Dhara said. 'She's insisted I say a few words, too. Wish me luck. Hmm – actually, wish *Ames* luck. I think he might faint.'

Zare watched his sister move gracefully through the crowd to the governor's side. Dhara was right, as usual. The year would pass and then he'd be with her at the Academy, helping bring security and prosperity to Lothal and the other planets of the Outer Rim.

He had no idea that everything was about to change.

PART 1:
AUTUMN

Zare decided he'd survive his year at AppSci the day Coach Ramset named him centre striker on the grav-ball team. Which was also the day he met Merei.

Practice was over, but Zare was still sitting on the lowest level of the stands in his pads and armour, peering down at game footage on his datapad with a grav-ball resting between his feet. He paused the footage and closed his eyes, letting the smell of cut grass fill his nostrils. Maintenance droids were simultaneously mowing the grid and repainting the green-and-white SaberCats logo in its centre, chattering at each other when their duties conflicted.

'Congratulations on being named centre striker,' someone said in a Core Worlds accent.

Zare was familiar with the clipped, superior tones

of the Core, but he'd rarely heard that accent since arriving on Lothal. He opened his eyes and saw a pale, skinny girl with short black hair looking down at him.

'Thanks,' Zare said, trying to recall if he should know her name. 'I'm Zare.'

'I know. What game were you watching?'

'Last season's final Carvers game,' Zare said. 'We play them this weekend. I've been trying to figure out their patterns. By knowing our opponents, we can hit the grid feeling like we've already played them.'

The girl looked sceptical.

'What's wrong?' asked Zare, a bit annoyed.

'It's not the same team – half the Carvers have graduated.'

'What's your name again?' Zare asked, now more than a bit annoyed.

'Merei Spanjaf – from your crop management class.'

'Of course,' Zare said. 'I remember now.'

'No, you don't,' Merei said, plopping herself down next to him. 'But that's OK. Go on – you were telling me your big plan.'

Zare raised an eyebrow at that, then shrugged.

'I'm scouting the Carvers' coach – not the players. He's still the same, right? Coaches don't change their strategies much from one year to the next.'

'Interesting hypothesis,' Merei said. 'Are you testing it, or just assuming you're right?'

'I'm watching the footage, aren't I?'

'And you know your eyes aren't deceiving you? You're sure you haven't started out with an idea and paid more attention to the facts that fit than the ones that don't? Because we do that all the time without realising it.'

'How would you do it, then?' Zare asked. 'Since you seem to think I got named centre striker despite being blind?'

'Oh, don't be a baby, Zare,' Merei said with a grin. 'Since you asked, I'd classify all the available grav-ball plays, then watch the footage and assign each play to a category, noting the score, position on the grid, and which drive of the series it is. But don't just do it for last season – that's too small a sample. Do it for all the seasons under the same coach. Then you'll have real information. Gut feelings are useful, but data is truth.'

Zare crossed his arms. 'And how did you learn so much about grav-ball?'

'By loving it my whole life,' Merei said. 'And before you ask, yes, I play. On Corulag I was top kicker in our youth bracket.'

'Corulag, huh? That explains the accent. When did you move to Lothal?'

'A little over a year ago. And you?'

'Beginning of the summer.'

'And do you like it here?' Merei asked.

'Yes,' Zare said, and realised he meant it. 'It's not a space station – that's an improvement right there. We've lived all over the place, assisting sector ag ministries with research projects. I hope we get to stay here for a while. I like the sunshine. And the air.'

'I like those things, too,' Merei said. 'How about the people?'

'They seem nice enough,' Zare said warily.

'Yeah, mostly,' Merei said. 'But some of the old-timers resent newcomers. They think we're all Core Worlders come to exploit them and tell them they're doing everything wrong. Which is true sometimes. But they love grav-ball – and that counts for a lot if you ask me.'

'What variant did you play?'

'Corellian rules. We played indoors, but the grid was the same size as this one.'

'Did you wear hover boots?' Zare asked.

'Never,' Merei said, looking offended. 'That's not real grav-ball.'

Zare must have looked sceptical, because Merei rolled her eyes.

'Oh, just gimme the ball,' she said.

Zare flipped the ball to Merei, who tucked it under

one arm and strolled out onto the grid, pausing to push her hair away from her face.

Under the rules played on Lothal, a grav-ball grid was divided lengthwise into eight zones, called octets. The team that won the chance-cube toss started at the centre of the grid. They had three drives to move eight meters into the next octet. Succeed and they got three new drives to go another eight metres. Fail and the ball went to the other team, going the other direction.

At either end of the grid was a scoring circle, and at the centre of that circle was the goal, a three-metre hoop on a stalk. Putting the ball through the goal by hand or tossing it through from inside the scoring circle was a touch-score, worth four points. Kicking it through the goal from anywhere on the grid was a kick-score, worth two.

The centre striker started each play with the ball. He or she could run with the ball, pass it to one of the two other strikers, or hand it to one of the two fullbacks for a carry. Behind the centre striker, two defenders and a keeper protected the goal.

Grav-ball was an exhausting, frantic game, with the same players having to alternate offence and defence over three periods. Zare loved the sudden shifts in momentum, the strategies and the satisfaction of outguessing or outplaying an opponent. And here on Lothal he'd discovered he loved it even more played on green grass and under a real sky.

Merei looked down the grid to the goal, nearly thirty metres away. She tossed the ball into the air and drove her foot into it, letting out a huff of effort. Zare watched the ball sail through the goal. It bounced off a maintenance droid, which let out an indignant squeal.

'Good kick,' Zare said when they stopped laughing. 'It's a bit harder with defenders in your face, but good kick. Were you on the squad last year?'

Merei shook her head.

'I don't like Ramset's play-calling,' Merei said. 'He's too conservative – it's mostly carries and he nearly always goes for the trap-kick on third drive, even when he's within a meter or two of gaining a new octet.'

Zare nodded, keeping his expression neutral. The kicker spent much of the game on the sidelines, coming in when the team needed a kick-score or a trap-kick – kicking the ball to the other team as far down the grid as possible.

Coach Ramset's conservative ways had bothered him throughout try-outs. But he wasn't going to tell this strange, pushy girl that.

'Maybe,' Zare said. 'But remember Coach only gets

one time-out per triad – the centre striker runs the offence. So what would you do differently?'

'Everything,' Merei said. 'You're the best player – you've got an accurate arm and you can improvise plays under fire. Ramsy was right to make you centre striker, at least.'

'Thanks,' Zare muttered, but Merei either didn't notice or ignored him.

'You've got two speedy strikers with good hands in Bennis and Kelio, and a solid defender in Atropos,' she said. 'Fullbacks are a little slow off the mark, though Sina's got a nice sense of the field. As for Ollet, he has good size – he ought to be better than he is. But Plandin is an average keeper at best, and Lazar doesn't have the range to be kicker. Point is, you should be passing more often to take advantage of your speed, with carries to keep the other guys honest. An offence that uses mostly carries makes sense if you've got bigger fullbacks and a keeper who can prevent scores. But you don't.'

Zare frowned, running a hand through his close-cropped hair. He still wasn't sure he liked this girl, but her scouting report of the SaberCats matched his.

'And your opinion of Coach Ramset is based on classifying plays, right?' he asked. 'Not just your eyes? Because you've told me those can't be trusted.'

'I looked at eight seasons' worth of footage,' Merei

said. 'I'll show you the percentages if you like. Or, if you prefer, I could crunch the numbers on the Carvers and see what strategies come to mind.'

'The game's in three days,' Zare said, trying not to let Merei hear that he was impressed. 'You can really do all that by then?'

'How's day after tomorrow?'

'OK,' Zare said. 'I'll look. But on one condition – you try out for kicker.'

Merei grinned and nodded.

Zare's agricultural-science classes were boring, but the class he really hated was Current Events.

It had sounded good; he'd imagined classroom discussions of the latest reports from the battlefield, with details about slavers and pirates earning their just rewards under the guns of the Imperial Navy. Instead the instructor, Mr Tralls, droned on about Imperial projects on planets Zare had never heard of. He spent most of his time in Current Events poking at his datapad or staring at the recruiting poster for the Imperial Academy and wondering what his sister was doing.

But one morning Zare heard Tralls mention the planet Chrona and looked up, startled.

'Chrona was where the Trade Federation helped

engineer a famine,' he said. 'They suppressed harvests of crops genetically modified to deliver more nutrients because a healthier population would need fewer medical services – on which they had a monopoly. Productivity on Chrona suffered for years until the Empire nationalised agriculture and reintroduced the modified . . . Do you have a question, Mr Leonis?'

'Yes, sir,' Zare said. 'Um, I'm sorry, sir, but what you just said isn't correct.'

Heads turned and his fellow students peered curiously at Zare.

'Is that so? What, exactly, was incorrect?'

'Well, sir, the Trade Federation had developed its own modified crops, but they weren't ready for mass production. They didn't care about medical services, just their own profit margins. And it was only a year before the new crops were distributed, after the Republic settled the court case in the Trade Federation's favour.'

A couple of students murmured. Tralls blinked at Zare, a stiff smile on his face.

'It seems Mr Leonis has other news sources than his teacher's, class,' he said. 'Though perhaps we should inquire into where he got this information? Well, Mr Leonis?'

'My parents developed the crops that the Trade Federation suppressed,' Zare said. 'They lived on

Chrona and testified before the Republic judiciary. My father still complains about the verdict all the time.'

Tralls was silent for a long moment. Someone in the back row laughed.

'But there wasn't any famine, sir,' Zare said. 'My parents would never have pursued the case if it meant people went hungry.'

'I see,' Tralls said. 'That was certainly enlightening, Mr Leonis. We'll discuss it further after class.'

Zare nodded, suddenly aware he'd done something wrong. He felt his cheeks flush.

After the other students filed out, Tralls looked him over, eyes cold.

'Do I draw up plays for you on the grav-ball grid?' he asked.

'No, sir,' Zare said.

'Then perhaps you'll do me the courtesy of not trying to teach my class.'

'But what you said –'

Tralls folded his arms across his chest.

'Do you wish the Trade Federation were still in business, Leonis?' he asked.

'No! They tried to ruin my family's work! But –'

'Then perhaps you might think about the point of today's lesson,' Tralls said. 'It wasn't to exactly represent the motives of a discredited organisation in a case that happened years ago, but to demonstrate how that organisation's actions affected the galaxy in the absence of a strong central authority. Progress was impeded, and the welfare of galactic citizens suffered. Do you disagree with either of those points?'

'No, sir,' Zare said. 'Of course not.'

'I'm glad we've established that,' Tralls said. 'Then before you raise your hand next time, think about whether your contribution is a positive one. Dismissed.'

'You can *do* this, SaberCats,' urged Coach Ramset, his red eyes bright in his green face. 'You've got to dig deep and find what's inside. Second drive, six metres to the next octet. Get a new set of drives and we'll have Merei in range for a kick-score and the win.'

The Duros coach clapped his hands as a cheer rose from the stands behind them. 'Two minutes left, Sabers. Let's do this!'

'Right,' said Zare, gulping water on the sidelines, huddled up with his teammates as the final seconds of their coach's final time-out ticked away. Beck Ollet was bleeding from a cut on his forehead, Frid Kelio's Rodian features were mottled dark green with fatigue, and Claith Bennis was gasping for breath. But all nodded at Coach Ramset.

'We're going one-eighty-three omega,' the Duros

coach said.

Zare nodded. That play called for faking a carry to Beck but giving the ball instead to Hench Sina, the beefy, tusked Aqualish who was the SaberCats' weak-side fullback.

He felt Merei stiffen beside him and glanced over. She was rigid with disapproval, feeling the play was too cautious.

'You heard Coach,' Zare said, giving Merei a warning look. 'Let's do this.'

The SaberCats walked back to their positions on the grid, cam droids drifting after them. A roar went up from the stands, which were packed with AppSci students and adults in green and white. Zare had expected a handful of onlookers, and been surprised to find the seating bowl around the grid almost completely full.

He looked at the SaberCats' wing attackers, waiting downfield outside the scoring circle; they weren't allowed inside it without the ball. He glanced at the Carvers across the drive line, waiting for the play to begin. Then his eyes jumped to the scoreboard: APPSCI 36 WEST CAP CITY 36.

Go for four, settle for two, Zare thought. *Make it happen.*

Beck and Hench crouched down in front of him and

he yelled, 'March!' Beck faked turning to take the ball as Zare pressed it into Hench's hands, then shoved the brawny Aqualish forwards into the Carvers. The two of them chugged forwards, feet digging at the grass. They gained two metres, then maybe one more. Then impact, pain, and stillness.

He heard the groan from the stands and knew before he even looked up: they were short of the next octet, with just one drive left. If they failed to gain three metres on this next play, they'd have to surrender the ball.

Zare looked over at Coach Ramset, saw him point to his foot and send Merei onto the grid, replacing Bennis. Ramset wanted the trap-kick: Merei would kick the ball deep to the Carvers, forcing them to begin their own attack with a long way to go and a minute and a half remaining.

Merei joined the huddle and Zare clapped her on the shoulder.

'Trap-kick offence, boys – keep them off our kicker,' he said. 'Then we'll stop them on defence.'

'Zare, it's not going to work,' Merei said. 'You're all tired, and their wing attackers have been outrunning us all day. They'll score and we won't have enough time to go back down the grid to tie.'

'You're not the coach,' Zare said.

'But you know I'm right,' Merei said. 'We've *studied* the Carvers, Zare. They always guard against a pass on this play and send defenders to the strong side. *Every time.*'

'I'm not tired,' Beck protested, but his pale face was flushed and his light blond hair was dark with sweat.

Zare glanced at the scoreboard, frowning. Then he nodded at Merei.

'I'm glad you're not tired, Ollet,' he said to Beck. 'Because you're getting the ball. I'm going to fake to Merei and send you up the weak side, with me and Sina blocking. We'll get a new set of drives, use up the clock, and kick for the win. But we've got to make the Carvers *believe* the fake. We've got to *sell* it. Now let's go!'

The SaberCats clapped hands and settled into their positions. Zare looked over Hench's shoulder at the Carvers. Their eyes were on Merei, behind him in position to kick. He bellowed, 'March!' and felt Beck duck behind him. He thrust the ball into Beck's outstretched hands and rammed his shoulder forwards, alongside Hench. He felt the crunch of impact, the Carvers defending them stumbled, and then they were chugging down the grid with Beck in the middle as the crowd roared. Ahead of him, the Carver defenders rushed to intercept, the keeper crouched to defend the goal.

The scoreboard told him there was one minute and eighteen seconds left in the game.

'OLLET, GET OFF THE GRID!' Zare yelled as he and a defender came together with a crunch of armour.

If the SaberCats scored too quickly, the Carvers would get the ball back with plenty of time to tie– and the SaberCats were too tired to stop them. Lying in the grass entangled with the Carver defender, Zare saw Beck take a hasty right turn and cross the boundary, ending the play and stopping the clock.

'Trick play,' the Carver player said disgustedly.

'You just wish you'd thought of it,' Zare said as he helped the other boy to his feet.

Lining up at the fifth octet, Zare glanced at the sidelines and saw Coach Ramset with his hands on his hips. Beside him, Merei grinned and pumped her fist. Zare saluted her.

'Carry plays,' he told his teammates. 'Keep it simple, burn up that clock, and give Merei a nice short kick for the win.'

The SaberCats were exhausted, but the Carvers were now demoralised. Zare and his teammates pushed through the fifth octet in two plays then ran two more plays that brought them near the end of the sixth octet, without risking a pass that a Carver defender might snatch out of the air. On the third drive, with two seconds left in the game, Zare turned and signalled for Merei.

Zare lingered under the sanisteam, letting the heat work the fatigue out of his muscles. He wound up leaving the locker room at the same time as Beck, who was pressing a spray-bandage over his forehead.

'Good game, man,' the big fullback said. 'Way to control the clock.'

'Thanks,' Zare said. 'Couldn't have done it without your big carry.'

'Or Spanjaf's kick,' Beck said. 'Where'd you find her?'

'More like she found me,' Zare said as they arrived at their parked jumpspeeders.

'Yeah, I bet,' Beck said, then grinned. 'She seems pretty capable.'

'Yeah, she does,' Zare said, wondering why he found Beck's smile suddenly annoying. 'We live on the west side. Where do you live?'

'Just this side of the marketplace,' Beck said.

'We're neighbours, then.'

'Guess so.' Beck frowned. 'I still can't keep Capital City straight. I grew up in the Westhills – ran a jogan orchard with my folks. We moved here in the spring. This town . . . it's a bit big for me.'

Zare nodded. 'Our last home was Hosk Station – I'm still getting used to looking up and seeing sky.'

Beck grimaced. 'Sounds awful.'

Zare shrugged. 'Just different. Why did you move?'

'Because the Empire was paying premium credits for orchards and farms,' Beck said. 'Guess I can't blame my folks for taking the offer, but I wish they hadn't. Still, the grav-ball grid here's a lot nicer than my old school's. Bennis said that's Fhurek's doing.'

'Fhurek?'

'Janus Fhurek – you've seen him talking to Ramsy on the sidelines. Skinny guy, kind of a red face. Bennis warned me that you don't want to get on his bad side.'

'So he's the headmaster, then?' Zare asked. 'But I thought the headmaster's name was . . .'

Beck brayed laughter.

'That's right, you're not from Lothal,' he said. 'Fhurek's the *athletic director* – around here that's a lot more powerful than headmaster. Think of this place as a junior sports organisation that also happens to be a school. Grav-ball every weekend in the autumn and winter, chin-bret every weekend in the spring – that's what puts the parents and the alums in the stands. And all the while, new ag specialists and Academy cadets are getting trained.'

'Academy cadets?' Zare asked.

'Sure,' Beck said. 'Fhurek's tight with the Academy administrators – a lot of officers have started off here. And a lot of stormtroopers, too, if that's what you want to do with your life.'

Zare shot his teammate an annoyed look.

'My sister's an Academy cadet,' he said.

Beck shrugged. 'No offence meant – I don't have anything against the Academy. It's just a little too regimented for me, that's all.'

'And then Merei sent it right through the goal. SaberCats thirty-eight, Carvers thirty-six, game over,' Zare said into his headset. 'You should have seen it, sis – it was beautiful.'

Dhara laughed, smiling at him over the datapad link.

'Sounds great. But was the coach mad that you didn't use his play?'

'Oh, I'd be in the soup if we'd lost,' Zare said. 'But we didn't. Thanks to Merei, and Beck.'

'And you,' Dhara said. 'I think you had something to do with it.'

'I suppose so,' Zare said, then grinned. 'How's the Academy?'

Dhara blew out her breath and rolled her eyes.

'I'm glad orientation is over and I can talk to you guys again. It's drills and more drills, and then some drills. Running drills, and agility drills, and weapons drills, and drills about drills. But I swear I'm already stronger and faster.'

'And tireder,' Zare said.

'Auntie Nags would say that isn't a word,' Dhara said. 'Seriously, though – it's hard but I like it. This is all I ever wanted to do – give back to the Empire. And now I get to do it.'

'And I'm still waiting.'

'Sounds tough, Mr Grav-Ball Star! Now tell me about this Beck. Have you got to know him at all? Or is he just the fullback?'

'I talked with him a little bit last night,' Zare said. 'He's third-generation Lothal – his parents just sold their orchard to the Imperial Agricultural Collective and moved here. I think he's a little homesick. He's almost as big as Ames, but . . . well, there's more going on upstairs.'

'Oh, don't be mean, Zare.'

'Sorry,' Zare said. 'How is Ames, anyway?'

'Good, I think,' Dhara said. 'I haven't seen him much since orientation, except during assessments. He's specialising in ground tactics and I'm mostly taking officer-training classes – there's an internship at Imperial headquarters that I really want to get. But I'll say hi for you next time I see him. Now I want to know about Merei.'

'What's to know? She came from Corulag with her family a year ago.'

'Oh? What ministry are they part of?'

'None – they're data-security specialists. Contractors to a bunch of ministries.'

'She'd love it here, then. Security is *crazy*. For instance, there are datapads that can't be taken out of certain rooms without a sensor firing and the whole Academy going on lockdown.'

'Merei would hate that,' Zare said. 'Unless we're on the grav-ball grid, she's never without her datapad. She's an information junkie.'

Dhara waited, then raised her eyebrows in that infuriating way she had.

'And that's it?' she asked.

'I don't know what you mean.'

'Oh, I think you do,' Dhara said. 'I get a feeling you like her.'

'She's my teammate,' Zare said, exasperated – and annoyed that his face suddenly felt warm. 'And my lab partner.'

'Sounds like you have chemistry together,' Dhara said.

That took Zare a second.

'And this sounds like I'm hanging up on you,' he said, as his sister laughed.

The next morning, Zare woke up to find a message on his datapad: Athletic Director Fhurek wanted to see him in his office during his first free period.

Zare walked down the path from the classroom building to the athletic complex. Fhurek's office was upstairs, above Coach Ramset's. The athletic director's walls were covered with commendations and holos, many of them showing him standing next to high-ranking local Imperials.

'Is that you, sir?' Zare asked, peering at a holo of a ruddy-faced young man in grav-ball armour.

Fhurek smiled.

'Good eyes, Leonis,' he said. 'Yes, that was forty-odd years ago. Fury Fhurek, they called me. Started at strong-side striker and moved up to centre striker. I held the AppSci record for completed passes until an alien broke it a few years ago.'

Fhurek looked at the image of his younger self for a moment, then smiled at Zare.

'But I didn't bring you here to relive my schoolboy heroics,' he said. 'Sit down, Leonis. First off, I wanted to congratulate you on being named centre striker, and the admirable leadership you've shown so far. I know you intend to enter the Academy next year, and I have friends in the administration – friends who appreciate the importance of the lessons we teach here in our athletics programs. I will make sure they know about what you accomplish at AppSci.'

'Thank you, sir,' Zare said. 'That means a lot to me. My sister's a new cadet this year and I can't wait to join her.'

'Dhara Leonis – I know,' Fhurek said. 'I hear she's doing well. Your family should be very proud of you both. And how is it playing for Coach Ramset?'

Zare's eyes skittered over the holos, his instinct for honesty and his loyalty to his coach briefly at war in his mind. But he knew the latter was more important.

'Well, we're still figuring out strategies and play-calling,' he said. 'But I like playing for Coach Ramset – everybody does. And he's a good teacher.'

Fhurek nodded.

'Good, good. What I've always loved about grav-ball is the coach teaches, but then it's up to the centre striker to win the game. In a way, it reminds me of what we're trying to do here on Lothal.'

'How's that, sir?'

'Ministers on Coruscant make plans for the Empire, but it's planets like Lothal where those plans are put into effect. Out here we're still ramping up production – of agricultural goods, of course, but also of minerals and other resources. At the same time, we're introducing the populace to the benefits of Imperial citizenship – and the responsibilities. We need to discover which alien and immigrant elements better our society, and which are undesirable. Quite a challenge, wouldn't you say, Leonis?'

'I suppose so, sir,' Zare said.

'You're new here – you'll understand soon,' Fhurek said. 'The point is, the future of the Empire will be built here, on planets like this one. In the Outer Rim we may lack some of the history and culture of the Core, but we're free to create a new order, one without the constraints of that past. That new order starts with the young, Leonis – at the Academy, but also right here on the grav-ball grid. The SaberCats are your team to help shape – your own new order to create.'

Zare hesitated. Yes, he was centre striker. But no centre striker ever won a game alone; it took a team to do that.

Fhurek saw his uncertainty and leant forwards, eyes fixed on Zare.

'I know that seems like a tall order, Leonis,' Fhurek said. 'And it demands both compassion and toughness. If I can help you figure it out, it would be my pleasure.'

The chime finally sounded just as Zare was convinced he'd actually fall asleep in Crop Management and get his first demerit of the year.

'I can't believe how boring that was,' he grumbled as he and Merei walked down the hall, passing AppSci students in a mixture of work overalls and SaberCats jackets. They'd become friends over the first month of school, progressing from nodding at each other when they passed in the hall to waiting for each other so they could catch up between periods.

'Boring?' Merei asked. 'Even the stuff about seeding clouds with enzymes? I thought the graph showing how nutrient output rose but then crashed was fascinating.'

'You're kidding, right?' Zare asked, holding the door open and following Merei into study hall. 'Nutrients, fertiliser . . . my parents love that stuff, but all I want is to get it over with and join my sister at the Academy.'

'I was talking about *information*, not farming,' Merei said as they sat at a table and pulled their datapads out of their satchels. 'Information is power – and just like on the grav-ball grid, you can use that power.'

'To do what? Maximise jogan-fruit yields?'

Merei looked around the room for a moment.

'Let me show you something,' she said. 'But not from my school account. I need to go through a service that makes me anonymous.'

'You're not going to do anything illegal, are you?' Zare asked.

'Shhh,' Merei said. 'Tell the whole Outer Rim, why don't you? No, nothing illegal – but I don't want anyone monitoring network activity to think otherwise.'

'What if you get caught?' Zare asked.

'Please,' Merei said. 'My mum and dad are data-security experts, remember? Give me some credit.'

Zare found himself watching her. She typed incredibly quickly, her fingers moving gracefully over her datapad without ever seeming to miss a key, and while he was still reading what was on the screen her eyes had devoured the available information and found the most important part, sending her fingers dancing across the keys again.

When he'd met her, he'd thought Merei was plain. But something about the way she arched her eyebrows made him want her to do it again. And then there was the way one corner of her mouth zoomed upwards right before she laughed. . . .

He shook his head.

Where did that come from?

'Whoever set up the Empire's network on Lothal was more concerned with speed than security,' Merei said. 'It's stuff like this that's been giving my parents heart attacks. Like AppSci's computers are linked to the entire Imperial network – not just the ag ministry, but transportation, security, and everything else. You can't see anything super sensitive, but look at this. These are records of TIE fighter patrols – assigned routes, flight duration, and so on. Now let's graph the flight paths on a map of the area around Capital City. Take a look.'

Zare saw a tangle of lines that looped between intersecting points.

'Here's us, and here's the main air base,' Merei said, gesturing at the datapad's surface. 'Now, look at the flight paths and take a guess where the fuel depots and recharge terminals are.'

'Here, here, and here,' Zare said, tapping the places where the loops converged.

'Three out of three,' Merei said with a smile and a wiggle of her eyebrows. 'Pretty good, Mr Leonis.'

'Thanks. But so what? Everybody knows where the depots are.'

'Everybody on Lothal knows. But someone from another star system could figure out the same information even if they've never set foot on this planet. Now look more closely at the flight paths. Guess which spots the Empire is most concerned about?'

Zare narrowed his eyes and pointed at several spots covered by multiple flight paths from different origins.

'Right again,' Merei said. 'You just found the Sienar flight lab, the governor's complex, and the ag ministry, and the minerals ministry – here comes Beck.'

Zare's eyes jumped among the points he'd identified.

'I see what you mean. But then what's at this point? And at this one out to the west?'

'I don't know,' Merei said, restarting her datapad. 'But whatever those things are, someone's pretty interested in them. Where have you been, Beck?'

Beck settled into the seat next to them with a sigh.

'Fieldwork,' he said wearily, closing his eyes. 'You spend the morning trying to administer a sedative to nerfs. I'm sure I stink.'

'I didn't want to say anything, pal, but that would be an accurate statement,' Zare said, wrinkling his nose at the sharp tang of nerf sweat clinging to the big fullback.

Beck shrugged. 'They don't call it Applied Sciences for nothing, you know. But yeah, I'll take jogan blossoms over a bunch of nerfs any day. The orchards on a warm autumn night? Sweetest smelling place in the whole galaxy.'

He frowned at the memory, his eyes far away. Which gave Zare an idea.

'Hey, Merei, AppSci's part of the ag ministry network, right?' Zare asked, trying to sound casual. 'Does that mean you can see information about the Ollets' old place?'

'I could call up general information for the area – crop yields and stuff like that,' Merei said. 'That part of the network is open to AppSci students for schoolwork.'

'I'd like to see that,' Beck said, standing to look over Merei's shoulder. 'Harvest begins in just a couple of weeks.'

'Perfect,' Zare said. 'You get to peek in on the old homestead and Merei gets to talk to someone who actually cares about farm reports.'

Merei stuck her tongue out at Zare but asked Beck for the coordinates and started tapping and clicking through menus with a speed neither boy could follow.

'This is where your family lived, right?' she asked.

'Yep,' Beck said, peering at the map. 'There's the river, and the hills, and the farmhouse is right here, in this valley. Hmmm. These are expected crop yields, right? They look low, but it was a dry summer with weird dust storms that rolled in from the west.'

Zare pulled out his datapad, thinking anything would be better than hearing Beck and Merei discussing crop yields.

'But what's this symbol?' Beck asked.

Zare peeked over at Merei's datapad. Beck was pointing at a blinking green cross. Merei pursed her lips and started typing.

'It's a land-use symbol,' she said. 'I found it – the area's been classified as 'RECODED FOR EXTRACTION/ REUSE."'

'That's got to be wrong,' Beck said. 'The jogan-fruit harvest is a tradition here.'

'I'm sure it is wrong,' Merei said. 'Probably some clerk in the ag ministry entered the wrong symbol. I'll flag it for review so they can change it.'

'Thanks,' Beck said. He looked at the screen and smiled. 'If we beat the Green Dragons this weekend, I'll take you out to see the orchards. You city kids need to see the real Lothal.'

The Green Dragons were no match for the SaberCats. Zare spent the whole day throwing to Bennis and Kelio for touch-scores, while Merei used well-placed trap-kicks to maroon them deep in their own territory. The SaberCats won by twenty-six, moving to 4–0 on the season, and as they came off the grid Fhurek locked eyes with Zare and pumped his fist. Zare grinned and saluted in response.

The next day, Zare met Merei and Beck on jumpspeeders. They donned their helmets and goggles and headed west. The mushroom-shaped bulk of Imperial headquarters and the other towers of Capital City shrank behind them and disappeared, leaving the three of them riding along the ferrocrete road through the grasslands, interrupted every few minutes by old landing beacons. Their towers were now abandoned, pitted with rust and creaking slightly in the wind.

The day was warm, and Zare enjoyed the way the wind rippled and dappled the fields, creating momentary patterns of light and dark green that ebbed and flowed around them. With Beck in the lead, they rode for about forty-five minutes, until hills appeared on the horizon. The hills grew until Zare could see they were covered with a mix of low shrubs and trees.

They topped a low rise and the land ahead dipped down to a white thread of fast-moving river that separated the grasslands from the hills beyond. A durasteel bridge spanned the river, barely wide enough to let a landspeeder pass. A ribbon of orange flexi-tape blocked the way across.

Beck eased up on the throttle and his jumpspeeder came to a halt. Zare raised his goggles.

'This is the Barchetta River,' Beck said, parking his speeder. 'And those are the Westhills on the other side. My family's orchards are right up there. But I don't know why the bridge is out.'

Someone had affixed a sign to the flexi-tape.

'"Scheduled for demolition,"' Beck said. 'It says to cross four kilometres south. But there's no bridge there.'

Something whined above, and Zare turned to see a trio of TIE fighters following the line of the river, perhaps a hundred metres above the water. He nudged Merei and the two of them waved at the fighters, cheering when the leader waggled his solar panels in response. They kept waving as the fighters shrank and disappeared to the south.

Beck was still scowling at the sign.

'They must have built a new bridge downriver,' Zare said.

'I guess,' Beck said. 'Only one way to find out.'

They followed a road along the river and soon found the new crossing, which was wide enough for a freight transport.

'See?' Zare asked.

Beck nodded, then looked upriver unhappily. 'I used to fish from that bridge with my pop. And now they're going to knock it down?'

Merei glanced at Zare.

'Progress means change, Beck, and that can be hard,' she said. 'The Empire will make your family's old lands feed more people. But that means you need bigger transports to bring the crops in for harvesting. And that means you need bigger bridges.'

'You don't have to talk down to me, you know,' Beck said. 'I may be out in the fields with the nerfs while you're crunching numbers, but we go to the same school.'

'I didn't mean –' Merei said.

'Forget it,' Beck said. 'Look, I'm glad the Empire's improving the harvest, but my family didn't just get here – when we planted the orchards you still carried a blaster because of Loth-wolves. So this isn't just numbers to me, Merei – it's home. Yeah, I get why they need a new bridge. But why can't they leave the old one, too?'

Beck shook his head. 'At least it's still the same river. Come on – even with the detour we're only a few minutes from the orchards.'

The Ollets' homestead was tucked in a hollow of the hills, behind a gate at the end of a pitted road. Beck lifted the latch on the gate and nodded for Zare and Merei to follow, leaving the jumpspeeders at the road.

'It's beautiful here,' Merei said.

Zare nodded. It was cool and shady under the trees, and the air was perfumed with something bright and sweet. Beck saw him sniffing and grinned.

'That's jogan blossom,' he said. 'Like I said, sweetest-smelling place in the galaxy.'

A rambling single-story house was set deeper beneath the trees, boarded up but intact. Beck stopped and looked at it for a moment, his chin quivering. Merei put her hand on his shoulder.

Zare started to say something, then paused. He'd heard a sound in the distance, like a twig snapping. As he turned to look, harsh barks erupted from beneath the trees. Several squat, yellow-furred creatures were running down the path towards them, sharp teeth bared. Spit flew from their mouths as they snarled and snapped.

'Look out – neks!' Zare yelped. But he realised almost immediately that it was too late; the speedy neks would reach them before they could retreat to the gate. He looked around frantically for something to hold them off – a stone or a fallen branch.

'Hold! Hold up there!' someone bellowed.

The neks came to an abrupt halt a few metres away from them and pawed the ground unhappily, growling. Behind them, a man in worn clothes came down the path, blaster rifle raised.

'Whoa, take it easy,' Beck said, putting his arms in the air. Merei and Zare did the same.

The man kept the rifle trained on them. He had lank black hair and a patchy beard.

'Who are you?' he demanded. 'You're trespassing.'

Beck put his hands on his hips. 'Beck Ollet. I lived here until the spring. I brought my friends from Capital City to show them where I grew up.'

The man frowned, then lowered the rifle. He whistled at the neks, who reluctantly trotted back up the hillside, turning to give Zare and his friends a last suspicious look.

'Grew up in Kinpany Gap myself,' the man said. 'They've started mining it now, y'know – everybody's sold out. Got a job providing security while the droid pickers are at work.'

'Droid pickers?' Beck asked. 'That work's too delicate for droids. And it's weeks too early to pick jogan.'

The man shrugged.

'I'm just here to guard the place. Look, I guess it's OK for you to look around a bit. But do it fast – I don't need any trouble.'

Beck nodded and led Zare and Merei up the path. After a minute they emerged in a field beneath the blue sky, one divided into neat lines of squat jogan trees. Maroon flowers drooped from the gnarled branches beside pale purple fruit that was criss-crossed with wavy white lines.

Black harvester droids were working their way down the trees, red photoreceptors peering at the fruit. Graspers snatched clumsily at the branches and cutting tools sheared away the fruit, which thudded into buckets.

'No, no,' Beck muttered. 'This is all wrong.'

Zare had never seen a jogan orchard, but he could tell immediately that Beck was right. One of the droids finished its work and backed away from a stripped tree, dragging its bucket behind it with one grasper. The ground was littered with broken branches and misshapen fruit.

'They're ruining everything,' Beck said, hands balled into fists.

'Beck, take it easy,' Merei said. 'We all know there's

no use arguing with droids. When we get back to Capital City we can file a report with the Ag Ministry. You can help them understand how to handle next year's harvest differently – how to make progress.'

'Progress,' Beck muttered, blinking as he looked over the ravaged orchard.

Beck was silent whenever Zare passed him in the halls of AppSci that week, but he took to the practice grid like he was possessed, levelling several of their teammates in drills. The week ended with a home game against the East City Brawlers, the fifth in the SaberCats season. Both Zare and Merei knew the Brawlers would be tough opponents: they had two burly fullbacks and a coach whose strategies followed no predictable pattern.

What Zare hadn't counted on was the ref.

In the last period, with AppSci up by two, Hench dropped the ball on a carry and Zare scrambled after it, wrapping it protectively in his arms as the Brawlers tried to pry it loose. He heard the chime indicating the play was over, got to one knee – and was driven into the turf by one of the East City fullbacks.

'What was that poodoo?' Beck roared at the offending Brawler, hauling a woozy Zare to his feet. The crowd was booing, and Zare could hear Coach Ramset and Merei screaming from the sidelines.

'Back to the line,' the ref said, a cam droid hovering over his shoulder. Zare had a sudden urge to smash the curious little machine.

'Sir, that's contact after the chime,' he said quietly to the ref. 'It's got to be a foul.'

'Maybe on whatever fancy planet you come from, kid, but on Lothal we call it smashmouth grav-ball,' the ref yelled, loud enough for the other SaberCats to turn and stare at him. 'Now get back to the line or I'll penalise you for an on-field delay.'

Zare looked at him for a moment, then turned his back.

'Huddle up!' he barked at his teammates. They stared at him through the protective bars of their green-and-white helmets. Beck was wild-eyed with fury.

'Don't let it rattle you,' Zare said, staring at each of the other SaberCats in turn. 'We're up by two, three minutes to go. Go down the grid for a touch-score and we're up by six and they're beaten. Or if we get the kick-score, they have to come all the way back for a touch to tie. Keep your cool and we've got this.'

The SaberCats marched down the grid, gaining hard-fought octet after hard-fought octet, until they were just outside the eighth octet and the scoring circle. It was third drive. Zare glanced at Bennis and Kelio, taking positions right outside the circle, with the

Brawlers' keeper flicking his eyes between them. Even if the SaberCats didn't score here, crossing into the eighth octet would give them three plays to try again.

'Sixty-four delta,' Zare said – he'd hand off to Beck behind the line and the fullback would either run it into the scoring circle for an attempted touch-score or heave it to Frid Kelio on the wing.

The SaberCats crouched down and Zare yelled 'March!' Bodies crashed into each other all around him and a Brawler threw him to the turf and landed on his back. He heard cheers and shoved the other boy away, getting to his knees to see Frid with his arms raised in triumph. The ball lay behind the goal and the Brawlers' keeper had his head down in despair.

Then Zare heard the cheers turn to gasps, and the sound of three chimes.

He turned and saw Beck on the ground, pummelling one of the Brawlers. Zare rushed to pull the fullback off the other player and got caught in a scrum, with everybody pushing and shoving.

'AppSci 23 is ejected!' the ref screamed, pointing at Beck. 'Major misconduct foul! That means no goal – East City gets the ball at centre grid!'

'It was a late hit!' Beck roared at the man. 'You saw it! Just like you saw the last one! You're crooked as a kriffing Hutt!'

'Off the field, 23!' the ref yelled. 'Or I'll have you suspended!'

Zare grabbed the back of Beck's uniform and started hauling the enraged fullback away from the play, signalling Coach Ramset for a substitute.

'You can't lose your cool like that,' he said to Beck. 'You just can't!'

'We're just supposed to sit there and get fouled? There's no point playing if the game's rigged, Zare!'

Three plays later, with a simmering Beck watching from the sidelines, a Brawler stiff-armed Hench, leapt over Zare's outstretched arms, and raced down the grid for an easy score as time expired.

Visiting Day at the Imperial Academy meant Zare had to cram himself into a formal tunic and endure both his mother and Auntie Nags attending to his hair despite his protests.

'Mum, enough!' Zare yelped. 'We're going to see Dhara, not the Emperor!'

'You are a prospective cadet,' Auntie Nags scolded, photoreceptors flashing yellow. 'That means you must look your best!'

Zare finally managed to escape the nanny droid, and half an hour later he and his parents walked through the main entrance of the Imperial Academy, accompanied by other parents and siblings looking equal parts nervous and proud. Then protocol droids ushered the visitors into an amphitheatre hung with banners emblazoned with the Imperial sigil. The anthem of the Empire began to play and everyone got hastily to their feet as cadets marched onto the stage from either side in immaculate white uniforms, grey trousers, and black boots.

Zare was the first to spot Dhara, but as always she'd already spotted him. Zare didn't know how she did that. When they were kids he'd refused to play hide-and-seek with her because she'd find him almost instantly. A grin split Dhara's face as she saw her brother pointing at her and she winked before resuming her serious expression.

After Commandant Aresko finished speaking, the cadets filed off the stage and joined their guests. Zare waited until his parents had greeted Dhara, then hugged his sister. She stepped back, smiled, then squeezed him again.

'It's only been a month but I swear you're taller,' she said. 'Must be all the grav-ball heroics.'

'No heroics yesterday,' Zare said, still fuming about the loss to East City.

'Mom told me,' Dhara said. 'Win or lose, you'll be glad for it – you may not think of it this way, but you're already training to be an officer. Teamwork, leadership, strategy, discipline – that's what we're taught here every day.'

'At least we get to talk to you,' Tepha Leonis said. 'Pari Bunkle hasn't been able to speak with Ames since he entered stormtrooper basic training – and she was told she couldn't visit.'

Dhara nodded. 'Stormtrooper training is crazy stuff. Glad I didn't get chosen to specialise in it. Though if I ever have to lead troops into battle, at least I'll know what it was like to wear a bucket and armour.'

'That's right,' Leo said. 'You'll know what you're asking your soldiers to do. That makes for a better leader.'

'Don't talk about war, either of you,' Tepha said. 'I want you nice and safe, Dhara, and far from any kind of battlefield. And that goes for you, too, Zare.'

Zare rolled his eyes.

'But enough about the Academy,' Dhara said. 'I want to know what's happening at home. Sounds like you had an unhappy adventure out west, little brother.'

'Yes,' Tepha said with a sigh. 'Someone in the ag ministry's made a mistake. I followed up on the report that Zare's friend Merei filed, but I didn't get anywhere. They're insisting that area be recoded for mineral extraction.'

'We've been over this,' Leo said. 'It's a matter of perspective. Lothal's too far from the trade routes to ship jogan-fruit profitably, and there's enough supply already for local needs. That area's more valuable for mining.'

'I know what the numbers say, Leo,' Tepha said. 'But sometimes it feels like those numbers have no room for growing things, or people.'

Leo was shaking his head, becoming agitated.

'Like I told Zare, this is *about* people,' he said. 'It's about maximising Lothal's value for *all* Imperial citizens, not just those who live here.'

'Tell that to Beck,' Leo said.

'Invite him over and I will,' his father replied. 'The men and women who run the Empire have to think of the well-being of the entire galaxy, not just one planet – let alone one orchard. That's what your sister's learning to do here, and apparently it's what you need to do, too, Zare.'

The four were silent for an awkward moment.

'So *that* went well,' Dhara said with a laugh. 'Let's try again. How's Auntie Nags?'

Zare chuckled. 'I have to send her out of the room before I tell Mum and Dad about grav-ball practice. She says it sounds dangerous. And dirty.'

'I agree with her about the dangerous part,' Tepha said with a scowl. 'Fourteen-year-old children playing full-contact grav-ball? I'm all for sports as part of a good education, but people on this planet are crazy.'

'Oh, Mum, enough!' Zare moaned.

Dhara laughed again. 'Dirty and dangerous, huh? And which one of those does Auntie Nags consider worse?'

'I think it's a tie,' Zare said.

Before practice the next day, Zare stopped by Fhurek's office.

'Sir, do you have a minute?' he asked.

'Of course, Leonis,' the athletic director said. 'Sit down. Tough break against East City.'

'I'm not sure I'd call it that, sir,' Zare said. 'That's what I wanted to talk with you about. We had that game won, and then . . . well, and then Beck turned it into a defeat by losing his temper.'

'Passion is part of grav-ball,' Fhurek said.

'Right. I know that, sir. And I don't want to take that away from Beck – he needs it to be effective. But he can't lose control like that – it puts everything we've worked for as a team in jeopardy.'

'Yes,' Fhurek said. 'Teamwork, leadership, strategy,

discipline – a grav-ball squad needs all of them to succeed.'

Zare cocked his head, curious. Then he remembered: Dhara had said much the same thing at the Academy on Visiting Day.

'Leonis?' Fhurek asked. 'I was asking you which quality success starts with.'

'Oh? Sorry.'

Zare considered the question.

'Teamwork,' he said. 'An average team that works together will beat a good team that doesn't. Take Hench, for example. He may not have Beck's talent, but I don't need to worry about him when I call a play at the line – I know he'll do his job and execute, regardless of the score, the refs, or anything else.'

'Are you talking about the Aqualish?'

'Yes,' Zare said. 'Hench Sina.'

'Right, that's the name,' Fhurek said. 'He strikes me as a brute-force fullback and nothing more.'

'Really? I don't see Hench that way at all, sir.'

'Perhaps you need to watch more carefully in practice then, Leonis,' Fhurek said. 'Don't get me wrong – a fullback who'll smash his head into a durasteel wall is valuable, in his way. But to win week in and week out, you need players with not just passion but also tactical intelligence.'

Zare looked at the athletic director, puzzled. He'd come in here to discuss Beck, who'd lost a game by taking a stupid penalty, and instead Fhurek was running down a SaberCats player who'd done nothing wrong – and who'd shown Zare the very qualities Fhurek said the team needed.

'Right, sir,' Zare said. 'Anyway, I was wondering if you had advice for dealing with the discipline issue.'

Fhurek brightened.

'Certainly,' he said. 'I asked you which quality was the most important one for success, and you said teamwork. But that's not correct, Leonis. It's *leadership*. Players – people – need to be led. They need to be taught – to execute strategies, to be disciplined, but most of all to *obey*. Remind your players of that, and you shouldn't have any more problems. And if you think a player can't be taught, then you have to consider if you'd be better off without them.'

'I don't see any problem there, sir,' Zare said.

'I'm glad to hear it,' Fhurek said. 'But keep your eyes open – a good leader doesn't let affection for his players blind him to their shortcomings. You understand that, right, Zare?'

'Absolutely,' Zare said, thinking of Beck's abilities – and his anger.

'Good,' Fhurek said. 'Now go out there and lead.'

When he hit the grid, Zare called Beck over to the sidelines and warned him that he planned to ride him all week about not getting lured into fouls against the Thrashers, the SaberCats' next opponent. Beck rolled his eyes, but to Zare's relief the message seemed to get through: he was eerily calm in every practice that week, rehearsing plays with icy effectiveness.

When the next game began, Zare caught sight of the Thrashers' two long-armed wing strikers and he allowed himself a moment of worry. But their centre striker's throws were erratic and their fullbacks kept turning the wrong way and missing tackles. Beck, meanwhile, looked like a different player: he ignored all fouls and provocations while shoving his opponents around the field. Merei got the scoring started with a pair of early kick-scores, and by the third period the Thrashers were exhausted, shoulders slumped as Zare connected with Bennis or Kelio to gain a new octet or sent Beck or Hench rumbling across the grid. The final score was SaberCats 44, Thrashers 18, and it didn't feel even that close.

Beck joined the other SaberCats in singing the AppSci fight song on the speeder bus back to Capital City, but when Zare and Merei exited with their equipment bags, he surprised them.

'I was thinking of taking another ride out to the orchards,' he said. 'You two want to come along?'

'Are you sure that's a good idea?' Merei asked as they tossed their bags on the hover-truck with the other SaberCats' gear.

'I just want to take another look,' Beck said. 'It might be the last time. Besides, it's even more beautiful in the moonlight.'

Zare glanced at Merei and saw his own doubt reflected in her face. She raised an eyebrow and pursed her lips, and he knew what she was thinking: *If he's going to go anyway, maybe we can keep him out of trouble.*

'OK, but just a quick look,' Zare said. 'If I'm too late Auntie Nags will send stormtroopers out after me.'

'Great,' Beck said. 'I just need to get something from my locker. Meet you at the jumpspeeders.'

Lothal was even more beautiful at night; that much Zare had to admit. One of the moons hung low in the western sky, and above their heads the stars were spilled across the heavens like some deity had thrown them there. It was amazing to think that one government controlled all of that, and that Zare and his family were a small part of its efforts.

Construction droids had been at work; beyond the new bridge a widened road now led up into the hills, almost all the way to the Ollets' old homestead. The three friends walked their jumpspeeders along the old road and left them outside the gate. Choruses of insects filled the darkness with song, and the silhouettes of night-hunting avians swooped across the stars.

Beck took a clear polybag out of his jumpspeeder's cargo carrier. Zare saw it was full of meat.

'Dosed with nek sedative,' Beck explained when he saw his friends' curious expressions. 'Relax – I just want to be able to look around without getting tooth marks on us.'

He lifted the gate and motioned for Merei and Zare to follow. The path leading to the orchard was a pale thread in the moonlight.

Merei was the first to see the shadowy figures moving down the lines of the jogan trees. But these weren't neks – they were people. When the intruders heard Merei's startled cry, they raced for the deeper woods to the south, crashing through the jogan branches as they went.

Zare squeezed Merei's shoulder, suddenly aware of how close she was to him. She looked up at him, their faces just a few centimetres apart, then turned away.

Zare started to say something, but saw Beck had moved into the orchard and was crouched beside a dark shape.

'Come on,' Zare said to Merei. In the moonlight he could see the dark shapes were squat droids, apparently deactivated. They had powerful arms that ended in flat metal discs.

'Those aren't harvester units,' Zare said.

'No, they're seismic surveyors,' Merei said. 'They use their instruments to create a 3-D map of the rock formations beneath the surface.'

'Your parents said this area had been reclassified for mineral extraction,' Beck said to Zare. 'I just didn't think it would happen this fast.'

'Me neither,' Zare said. 'But what are those things sticking out? Down low, on the droid chassis.'

'They're detonators,' Beck said, getting to his feet and looking down at the surveyor droid. 'Someone's rigged these droids to explode. There's no danger, though – whoever we interrupted didn't get a chance to set the primers.'

'Then we've got to tell someone,' Merei said.

Beck snorted. 'Let them blow.'

'You don't mean that,' Zare said. 'None of us like what's happening to the orchard, but this is illegal – and dangerous. I'm calling the authorities.'

'Fine, you do that, Zare,' Beck said. 'I'm going to go find the people who did this.'

'Are you crazy?' Merei hissed. 'You could get hurt.'

'Or mistaken by the authorities for one of the intruders,' Zare said.

'I'll be back before they get here,' Beck said. 'I spent my whole life in these woods, remember. I know every centimetre of them.'

He headed off across the orchard. Zare took his comlink from his belt and commed the emergency channel, telling the Imperial lieutenant who answered where he was and setting his comlink's locator so it could be tracked. Then he and Merei waited nervously in the darkness, only slightly reassured by the whine of TIE fighters somewhere in the night above them.

'Some adventure, huh?' Zare asked.

'It's a little too much for me,' Merei said, but she squeezed his hand. Despite his uneasiness, Zare smiled – and Merei smiled back, her face pale in the moonlight. He leant towards her.

Branches snapped and Beck appeared out of the darkness. Zare and Merei parted hastily, but apparently not hastily enough.

'So you're going to be his girl, I guess,' Beck said.

Merei crossed her arms over her chest. 'I'm my own

girl, thank you very much,' she said.

Zare was grateful when lights appeared at the far end of the orchard. The three of them shielded their eyes as the troop transport turned a spotlight on them.

Zare stepped forwards as the stormtroopers disembarked from their side-mounted compartments, but Beck got there first.

'They went that way,' he said, and pointed to the forests to the north.

Zare started to protest that Beck was sending the soldiers the wrong way – the intruders had run south – but stopped at the grim expression on his friend's face.

'Fan out, men – search formation,' the squad leader said, his electronically modulated voice harsh in the night. 'You kids get back to your bikes and head home. We'll take it from here.'

When they got back to Capital City's marketplace, now shuttered for the night, Beck simply raised his hand in a curt farewell and zoomed off towards his own house.

Merei watched him go, teeth worrying at her lip.

'Was he worried about the intruders?' she asked, then looked around and lowered her voice. 'Or worried someone might catch them?'

'I couldn't tell,' Zare said.

'I don't think I want to go back out there,' Merei

said. 'And I don't think the two of you should, either. I'm scared something bad is going to happen if you do. It's strange – I don't get worried poking around networks, even when I know I'm investigating things I probably shouldn't be, and it would be bad if I got caught. But to have it happen out here, in the real world? That felt totally different.' She took off her helmet, shaking her head. 'Now you think I'm ridiculous.'

'That wasn't what I was thinking at all,' Zare said. 'About the other thing, Merei . . .'

Merei took a sudden interest in fixing the strap on her goggles.

'I'm sorry, Zare, I . . . I don't want things to be weird,' she said, the words colliding and tripping over each other in her haste. 'We're . . . we're teammates.'

'And friends,' Zare said.

'And friends,' Merei said. 'I want us *all* to be friends.'

'I want that, too.'

'Right, OK.' Merei crammed her helmet back on. 'So I'm glad we settled that. Good night, Zare.'

The lights of her jumpspeeder shrank and vanished in the darkness, leaving Zare to wonder what, if anything, they'd settled.

★ ★ ★

Auntie Nags woke Zare the next morning, her photoreceptors yellow.

'An Imperial officer is at the door,' she said. 'He wants you to come with him to the security ministry for questioning.'

Zare sat up in bed, instantly awake. He fumbled for his clothes while Auntie Nags rolled back and forth in agitation.

'Are Mum and Dad here?' Zare asked.

'Yes. They've offered our visitor a cup of caf.'

Auntie Nags's eyes flashed red.

'How could you, Zare Leonis? This is related to that foolish *adventure* you and your friends went on last night, isn't it? The one you told your parents about when you arrived home at an improper hour.'

'Remind me not to thank whoever programmed you for eavesdropping,' Zare muttered. 'Since you heard that, you also heard me say we didn't do anything wrong.'

Auntie Nags rolled away grumbling something. What he'd said was true, Zare told himself – they *hadn't* done anything wrong, at least not really. And he'd told his parents the truth. Or most of it, anyway – he'd decided not to mention the detail about Beck sending

the stormtroopers in the wrong direction.

Zare went into the kitchen and found Lieutenant Roddance drinking the last of his caf. The officer nodded at Zare and got to his feet.

'As I've told your parents, you're not in trouble,' Roddance said. 'In fact, you're to be commended for alerting the Security Ministry to a potential insurrection. I just need you to come with me and tell us what you saw. It's to assist our investigation.'

Zare nodded, and at the Security Ministry he did as Roddance asked, telling the lieutenant everything – except, once again, what Beck had done.

PART 2: WINTER

Since he'd spent most of his childhood aboard space stations, Zare was unprepared for the arrival of winter on Lothal; he'd accompanied his parents to planets that felt too hot, too cold, or just right, but it seemed bizarre to have the same planet change temperature. If not for Auntie Nags's built-in weather sensors, he would never have remembered to take a coat to school.

It rarely if ever snowed on Lothal, but in the winter the grasslands turned pale green mixed with brown, and the winds blew hard from the west. As autumn turned to winter, those winds brought more and more dust, which left everything wearing a fine coat of tan – and long-time residents grousing that the dust storms were peculiar.

The winter also brought exams, which meant two

weeks with few grav-ball practices and no games. During review periods Zare found himself staring out the classroom windows. Somehow he preferred trying to catch sight of the grid to boning up on the dynamics of water retention in various soil types. These daydreams inevitably ended with an elbow in the ribs from Merei.

Merei admitted she hadn't told the Imperials about Beck misleading the stormtroopers, either. Beck, for his part, avoided his friends' questions, curtly telling them that he had to study.

As the weather cooled, the tension that had settled over the three of them ebbed as well, though it never really vanished. When Zare was in the same room with Merei, or on the grid with her in practice, he was always aware of the slightest movement she made; if she touched her hair or turned her head his senses alerted him to the change. And Zare frequently caught Merei glancing in his direction during quiet moments, then hurriedly looking away when their eyes met.

His parents knew none of this, and when Dhara enquired, he changed the subject then tried to ignore her delighted laughter. But the incident in the orchards remained a stubborn topic of discussion at home, with Zare's father often muttering darkly about Separatists and splittists.

'This insurgency is a disease,' he said over breakfast, one hand coming down on the table hard enough to rattle the plates. 'It's the same selfishness that left the Republic weak and useless, prey to the Separatists and their mechanical murderers.'

'Oh, that's crazy, Dad,' Zare said.

His mother and father looked at him in surprise – and in truth he'd surprised himself.

'Why is that crazy, Zare?' his mother asked.

'Yes, Zare,' Leo Leonis rumbled ominously. 'I'm curious to hear why you've become a supporter of disorder.'

'Whoever tried to blow up those droids wasn't trying to kill anybody,' Zare said. 'I think they were just frustrated – and looking for a way to protest.'

'That's not the way civilised beings protest,' his father said. 'And what are they protesting, exactly?'

'Seeing their farms turned into mines, for one thing.'

Leo shook his head. 'Not this again. Did your friend Beck's parents have their land seized?'

'No,' Zare admitted.

'Ah. So they sold it voluntarily, for a fair price?'

'They wouldn't have sold it if they knew what the Empire was going to do with it,' Zare said angrily. 'And I think their neighbours feel the same way.'

'Zare,' his mother said with a warning look at her

husband. 'You know I feel the same way you do about that land. I tried to convince the Ag Ministry that it was making a mistake, remember? But blowing up equipment is violence. And protests and civil disobedience inevitably lead to violence, too – violence and anarchy.'

'I don't believe that,' Zare said. 'If a protest makes the Empire realise a policy is bad, doesn't that make the Empire stronger?'

'Not in the real world,' Leo said. 'Such things only create opportunities for evil people to exploit for their own purposes, Zare. Please believe us – we've seen it happen. The best minds of the galaxy work for the Empire – and while mistakes do get made, in the end the Empire figures out the correct policies. The way to make the Empire stronger is to trust in the experts, learn from them, and be patient.'

With the long grind of exams left behind, it was a relief to return to the grav-ball grid, which the maintenance droids had kept lush and green even as the fields of Lothal turned pale and dry.

The SaberCats' first game back was against the South Capital City Volunteers, and took place at AppSci in a cold drizzle. The stands were full anyway: the SaberCats' first-half record meant a trip to the league championships was a possibility. Zare's parents were huddled under a stasis field, near Athletic Director Fhurek.

The Vols won the chance-cube roll and started with the ball. Before first chime it started to rain harder, the cold raising bumps on Zare's arms.

'And to think you wanted exams to be over so you could get out here again and enjoy this,' Zare told his miserable teammates in the huddle.

His teammates grinned, and Hench removed his tusk-guard and chuffed laughter.

'Be alert for trick plays – the Vols love to hand off to their weak-side fullback and then have him pass deep to the strikers,' Zare reminded them.

The chime sounded and the SaberCats grunted as they came together with their opponents with a crunch of armour, Zare lurking behind the line, waiting to plug a hole in the defence. He leapt in the air and batted away a low pass, shaking the rain from his helmet.

The Volunteers pushed the SaberCats steadily down the grid, gaining octets through a slow but effective combination of carries and short passes. But Atropos and AppSci's other defender, Roly Umber, kept them from securing a touch-score, forcing the Volunteers to settle for a kick-score and two points.

Standing at centre, Zare rubbed his arms in a futile attempt to get warm.

'OK, deuce-sixteen gamma,' he said.

'No fancy stuff, Zare,' grunted Beck. 'Just give me the ball.'

'Get back to the line, Beck,' Zare said sternly. 'The play is deuce-sixteen gamma.'

They gained four metres on the carry, then five on a short pass, carrying them into the next octet. Both teams' uniforms were already dark with mud.

'Three-twelve delta,' Zare said, and Beck nodded. That was a handoff to Beck, who'd follow Hench, tossing the ball back to Zare behind the line if Kelio or Bennis had an opening downgrid.

'March!' yelled Zare and slapped the ball into Beck's big hands. Hench broke right, grappling with a Volunteers defender and opening a hole for Beck to break further right and go up the sidelines. Then Zare saw Frid cut in front of the goal just outside the scoring circle while the Volunteers' keeper fixed his attention on Beck.

'Beck! Downgrid! Pass back to me!'

But Beck ignored Zare and chugged straight ahead, arm in front of him like a battering ram, his feet kicking up mud. The Vols' centre striker got his arms around him but Beck shrugged him off as the AppSci stands erupted in cheers.

Beck just kept going and was finally brought down just inside the seventh octet. Zare shook his head and trudged up to the new drive line with his teammates. Frid had left his normal position downgrid to join the huddle, wrinkling his snout in confusion.

'Did we change three-twelve delta?' he asked.

'One of us did,' Zare said, glaring at Beck. 'How about we follow the playbook from now on, Ollet?'

Beck just glared back.

'Like I said, Zare – just give me the ball.'

The SaberCats won by twelve, but Zare was too chilled and too annoyed with Beck to do more than lift a hand to acknowledge the cheers. Waiting on the sidelines, Coach Ramset pumped his fists in delight.

'Lots of plays changed at the line, Zare, but I won't argue with success,' Ramset said, wiping the rain off his bald green head. 'That's what happens when you play with passion! I don't know what got into you today, Ollet, but whatever it is let's have some more of it – you were like a runaway hover-train. And now Athletic Director Fhurek has a few words to say.'

Fhurek descended from the bleachers, his ruddy face shielded from the rain by a stasis cone attached to his AppSci cap. The SaberCats moved aside so he could stand in the centre of their circle. The raindrops bounced off the stasis cone's deflection field and into the players' faces, but Fhurek didn't seem to notice.

'You took no prisoners out there,' Fhurek said, nodding at Beck. 'I've always been a fan of smashmouth grav-ball – no trickery, just a question of who wants it more.'

Zare looked at the athletic director in disbelief. What had happened to tactical intelligence?

'Hench had a great game too, sir,' Zare said.

Fhurek's eyes jumped to the big Aqualish, whose hide was steaming in the cold rain. His face seemed to twist and he looked away. Zare risked a glance at Merei but found her face stony and unreadable.

'You all did,' Fhurek said, then smiled again. 'Keep it up and I see a shot at the league championship in this team's future. And that would do wonders for your prospects after graduation, wouldn't it?'

The SaberCats muttered agreement, thinking of hot sanisteams and the chance to go home.

Zare told his parents not to wait, and rode his jumpspeeder home at a measured pace so its repulsor lift wouldn't sling water on the pedestrians unfortunate enough to be out on a miserable night in Capital City. He was a block from the apartment when one of the people walking caught his eye: he was big and trudging along as if he didn't notice the rain or the cold.

Zare looked again, then stopped.

'Ames!'

He had to call twice more before Ames Bunkle came to a halt and looked to see who was calling his name. He regarded Zare for a moment, then nodded and walked slowly to the edge of the pavement. His hair was cut to a few millimetres in length and rain was running down his face and dripping off the end of his nose.

'Ames, it's me – it's Zare Leonis. What are you doing out here?'

'My mother,' Ames said, blinking slowly. 'She's ill. Two-day leave to see her.'

'That's right – Auntie Nags told me,' Zare said. 'She must be glad to see you.'

'Yes,' Ames said after a moment.

'And how are you, Ames?'

'DX-578,' Ames said.

'What did you say?'

'DX-578. My operating number is DX-578.'

For a moment Zare thought his neighbour was joking, but Ames had never been one for jokes.

'Of course,' Zare said. 'But since we're not at the Academy, I can call you Ames. That's OK, right?'

Ames considered the question.

'Yes,' he said.

'Dhara said you've been away on stormtrooper training,' Zare said. 'It must be hard work.'

'Yes,' Ames said. 'They wouldn't let me take my E-11 on leave. Blaster rifles are restricted to Academy grounds. I can field-strip it blindfolded now, you know.'

'I guess that'll be good if you ever go into combat blindfolded,' Zare said.

'Yes,' Ames said, and let the rain keep running down his face.

'It was a joke, Ames!'

Ames didn't say anything.

Zare turned back to his jumpspeeder, trying to think of a way to end the disturbing conversation. But then he turned back to where Ames was still waiting in the rain.

'Ames?' he asked. 'Do you like it? The Academy, I mean?'

'Yes,' Ames said. 'I'm serving the Empire.'

And then he smiled – the first expression Zare had seen on his face.

Dhara commed to congratulate Zare on the win, and sensed – as she always seemed to – that her brother wanted to talk to her without their parents on the feed.

After a few minutes catching them up on what was happening at the Academy, she raised one eyebrow and told their parents that she and Zare had to discuss preparations for Tepha's birthday.

Zare took his datapad into his bedroom and let the door slide closed behind him.

'How do you always know?' he asked Dhara.

'Because I'm a *sorceress*,' Dhara said, wiggling her fingers and laughing. 'I don't know, little brother. Maybe it's that what you're thinking is always so obvious. Now, what's on your mind?'

He told her about running into Ames and she nodded.

'Stormtrooper training is intense, Zare,' she said. 'They're turning boys – and a few girls, in case you didn't know – into soldiers. They do that by breaking them down, then building them back up as soldiers. It's essential training in following orders, understanding tactics, and executing plans as a team.'

Teamwork again, Zare thought. *But at what price?*

'Ames seemed like he wasn't all there,' Zare said. 'Like he was someone else.'

'Like I said, it's intense,' Dhara said. 'But it's also temporary. Ames is only halfway through the process. Look at me, has the Academy made me different?'

Zare shook his head.

'Good. I promise you I'm not being brainwashed or anything like that. And Mum would think this was a snobby thing to say, but I'm not going to be a stormtrooper and neither are you. Officer training is a lot different. You'll see.'

The SaberCats split their next two games, running their record to 7–2. The day before their tenth and final regular-season game, Zare's datapad beeped. Fhurek wanted to see him in his office immediately.

Zare arrived to find the athletic director behind his broad desk. Coach Ramset was hunched in a chair, looking down into his lap.

'You wanted to see me, sir?' Zare asked, looking at the Duros coach for any hint about what was going on.

'Sit down, Zare,' Fhurek said. He put his elbows on his desk and steepled his fingers. 'I'm afraid we're going to need some changes to the SaberCats' roster.'

Zare glanced at Coach Ramset, puzzled, but the coach didn't look up.

This is about Beck, Zare thought, fighting down panic. *Ramsy told him about Beck ignoring the playbook, and now Fhurek's embarrassed. Maybe he even knows about the incident at the orchard.*

'I think our roster's pretty good, sir,' Zare said carefully. 'We've got some weaknesses, but every team does. I know in our last game we had a little problem with discipline and sticking to the game plan, but it's nothing I can't handle. I feel like we've really come together as a unit over the last few games.'

Fhurek shook his head. 'Coach Ramset, perhaps you can explain the issue?'

Ramset looked from Fhurek to Zare, his face dark with misery. 'I wouldn't know how to put it, sir,' he said.

Fhurek's face darkened to an alarming purple. 'Very well, then. I'll do it. It's the alien players, Zare. Kelio and the other one . . . Sina. If we win this game, we're guaranteed a shot at the championship. But if that happens, those two will need to be removed from the roster.'

'What? Why?'

Fhurek smiled thinly. 'Because I said so, Leonis. I have no issues with aliens myself – some of my best friends are nonhumans – but some grav-ball fans object to alien physiognomies, seeing them as giving nonhumans an edge.'

'You want to kick Frid and Hench off the squad?' Zare demanded. 'They're important members of the team! They've earned this!'

'I don't *want* to do anything,' Fhurek said. 'As centre striker, it's your job to deliver a grav-ball title for the SaberCats. But as athletic director of AppSci, it's my job to make sure that title isn't . . . *tainted* by talk that we had an unfair advantage. Isn't that right, Coach Ramset?'

'I can see why misguided people might think that,' Ramset mumbled, and Zare felt his anger at the old Duros evaporate, replaced by pity. He was too scared to protest any more vigorously than this.

'That's the right word exactly, Coach – "misguided,"' Fhurek said. 'I couldn't agree more. It's a shame some people feel that way. But we shouldn't be worrying about social change – just winning that grav-ball title.'

'Which is more likely with Frid and Hench,' Zare said. 'There's no league rule against nonhuman players. How am I supposed to –'

'By *leading*, Leonis,' Fhurek snapped. 'You need your best team on the grid for the championship game. I'm sure your two nonhumans are fine individuals, but are you sure they have the necessary capabilities to grasp strategy and tactics?'

'I've told you they do!' Zare said, his voice rising. 'A minute ago they couldn't play because they were too good. Now it's because they're too stupid?'

'That's enough, Leonis! I'm an honourable man – Kelio and Sina can play tomorrow, but they're out by the championship game. I'll let the two of you decide how to break it to them.'

'You want leadership?' Zare asked. 'Then here it is: Coach Ramset and I spent the entire autumn making these players into the best possible SaberCats team. And that's the team that's going to play.'

And then he stormed out of the office.

'Obviously that man wasn't raised right,' sniffed Auntie Nags, her photoreceptors blazing red.

'Obviously not,' Leo Leonis said. 'That's the problem with the Outer Rim – small-minded thugs like this athletic director get little kingdoms to rule, when closer to the Core Worlds they'd have to compete with more qualified people, and would wind up fixing droids or cleaning streets.'

'Honestly, Leo,' Tepha said. 'Let's not blame the entire Outer Rim for the actions of one man.'

Zare's father muttered something.

'Zare, I agree this is awful,' Tepha said. 'But is it worth damaging your chances of getting into the Academy?'

'Oh, come on. Anyone can sign up for the Academy, Mother.'

'But they don't *accept* everybody. This isn't the time to make enemies, dear – and remember Athletic

Director Fhurek's connections at the Academy. He can only affect your life for a few more months – after that he'll have no power over you.'

'But he'll still have power over AppSci players! He'll still be able to do things like this!'

Tepha nodded, clearly troubled.

'And he shouldn't be allowed to,' she said. 'Your father may not agree with me about this, but there's too much of this *everywhere* in the Empire, particularly in the lower levels of the bureaucracy. Mean little men like Fhurek may not rise very high, but that's no comfort to the people whose lives they control.'

'Exactly,' Zare said. 'Somebody needs to stop them.'

'Unfortunately, an AppSci student isn't in a position to do that,' Leo said. 'People like Fhurek always get found out. Take comfort in that.'

'And what about Frid and Hench?' Zare demanded. 'How will that help them?'

Tepha shook her head. 'It won't, at least not now. And I hate that. But if you take on the athletic director you'll only wind up hurting yourself, Zare – and then you won't be able to help anybody.'

Zare stared down at his hands for a moment. Then he raised his eyes and nodded.

'I know what to do now,' he said.

'And what's that?' his father asked.

'You'll see,' Zare said. 'I can't stop Fhurek from doing this. But I can force him to make it clear to everybody *why* he's doing it.'

What made it worse was that Hench and Frid were the two SaberCats most excited about the chance to play for the title, reminding their teammates over and over again on the speeder bus to Forked River that it was 'win and we're in.' Zare sat in the front next to Merei, turning his helmet over and over in his hands.

When she asked him what was wrong, he just shook his head.

Zare already knew that the Mavericks weren't a good team; they were 1–8 on the season, and even in warm-ups Zare could see that their centre striker was erratic and their kicker didn't have enough range. But more than that, they had no discipline: their coach had to yell repeatedly to get them to listen, and at any point during pregame drills at least half the team was wandering around or chatting with spectators.

The SaberCats won the roll of the chance-cube and began on offence. Before Bennis and Kelio could trot down to their positions outside the enemy scoring circle, Zare called them back to the huddle.

'Frid, get ready to run,' Zare said. 'You're going to be busy today. You too, Hench.'

The Rodian and the Aqualish looked at each other, puzzled, then nodded.

'All right, SaberCats,' Zare said. 'Remember – win and we're in.'

The starting chime sounded and the Forked River fans began to cheer. Zare called the first play: handoff to Hench. Beck drove the opposing back for the Mavericks into the ground and Hench hurdled him, making it nearly to the next octet. Zare promptly called the same play again, and this time Hench crossed the octet boundary with a short gain.

'Eighty-three epsilon,' Zare said.

Every play was coded so the opposing team didn't know what was being called. Beck and Hench worked through the calculations in their heads, then looked at Zare in surprise. It was the same play.

'Eighty-three epsilon!' Zare repeated.

Hench bounced off Beck and rumbled to within a metre of the seventh octet.

'Get to the line,' Zare barked. 'We're not standing around today.'

'You gonna call any other plays in this game?' Beck asked.

'Yes – starting now,' Zare said, not caring if the Mavericks heard him. 'Three-niner gamma.'

That was a quick strike to Frid. Zare dropped back,

noting approvingly that his offence was holding the Maverick defenders at bay with little effort. Frid was juking and weaving in the eighth octet. Zare gauged the weak-side wing's speed, then fired the grav-ball on a line right at the Forked River keeper. Frid snagged it in front of the boy's face on the edge of the scoring circle, spun around the keeper, and slammed it through the goal for four points.

The Mavericks didn't make a single octet during their drive and the SaberCats recovered the trap-kick in the middle of the third octet. Zare immediately ordered a handoff to Hench. Then another. Then he fired a long pass in Frid's direction that went wide, caroming off the goal stalk and sending a cam droid diving out of the way.

A stuttering chime signalled a coach's time-out.

'Leonis!' Coach Ramset barked from the sideline. 'Get your team over here.'

Zare and his teammates assembled in front of the Duros coach.

'Not the most sophisticated game plan,' Ramset said. 'Switch to attack pattern beta – end sweeps and short passes to a mix of receivers. That's an order, Zare.'

Zare nodded, but as the SaberCats headed back onto the grid, Coach Ramset grabbed his shoulder.

'I know what you're doing,' he said.

'Good,' Zare said. 'Then you also know why I'm doing it.'

The SaberCats won by thirty-two and returned to AppSci knowing they were going to play for the league title. Hench Sina had broken Ames Bunkle's school records for carries and metres gained in a single game, while Frid Kelio had wound up two completions shy of tying another single-game mark.

A crowd of cheering students was waiting for the SaberCats' speeder bus. The SaberCats slapped hands with the students, grinning and joining impromptu choruses of the school fight song. But at the back of the crowd Zare spotted Fhurek, his eyes bulging with fury.

Zare took his time making his way through the crowd, then nodded at the man.

'Proud of yourself, Leonis?' Fhurek all but spat.

'Proud of my teammates, sir,' Zare said. Then he turned and raised his voice: 'Hey! Weren't Frid and Hench incredible?'

The students began cheering again. Fhurek pumped his fist in celebration, a sickly smile plastered on his face.

'We're going to play for the league championship!' Zare yelled.

When the commotion died down again, Fhurek leaned close to Zare, wagging his finger. 'If I had another centre striker, you wouldn't be playing next week.'

But you don't, Zare thought. *And we both know it.*

He started to walk past the athletic director to the locker room, but Fhurek caught him by the arm and spun him around.

'Enjoy your little stunt, Leonis,' Fhurek hissed. 'But you best watch yourself. You have no idea what I'm capable of.'

The day after the SaberCats beat Forked River, Zare was eating lunch at home when his comlink started beeping.

He ignored it, but when it happened a third time he looked apologetically at his parents and slipped away from the table, trying not to notice that Auntie Nags's photoreceptors had changed instantly from green to red.

It was Beck, and it took Zare at least a minute to understand what he was trying to say.

'Gone,' he kept saying. 'Everything's gone.'

'The orchards?' Zare asked, feeling sick to his stomach.

'Yeah,' Beck managed.

'And you're there now?'

'Yes.'

'OK,' Zare said. 'I'm coming. Don't do anything crazy. Just wait for me. Promise me, Beck. You'll just wait.'

'I'm not going anywhere.'

Zare raced west on his jumpspeeder, the cold air stinging the exposed skin beneath his goggles. Ten kilometres outside of Capital City, he caught up with a line of vehicles. The first was an Imperial troop transport, nearly silent on its efficient repulsorlifts. Zare passed the hulking transport, which was at the tail end of a convoy of ramshackle civilian speeders. They had belongings tied atop their roofs. Men and women behind the speeders' controls looked over at the boy on the jumpspeeder, their faces etched with misery. At the front of the line was another transport. The stormtroopers in their side compartments stared straight ahead, motionless. Zare accelerated, forcing himself not to look back at the strange procession until he was sure it was far behind him.

Zare stopped at the narrow bridge over the river to wipe the dust from his face. The river was dark, choked with dirt and debris. Zare peered over the parapet and saw dead fish floating everywhere, swollen and white.

Ahead, he saw the hills were crowned with greasy-looking black smoke.

He crossed the river at the new bridge and found Beck's jumpspeeder at the turnoff to the Ollet homestead. The garden gate was gone. So was the house. A ferrocrete road had replaced the path up the hill, and empty pits and churned-up soil marked where the trees had been.

He found Beck at the top of the hill, seated on a boulder still dark with soil where it had been pried out of the ground. He was looking out at what had once been his family's orchard. Where the trees had been Zare saw stacks of construction equipment. He could hear thumping from the other side of the hills and a whine that rose and fell, making his head hurt.

'Are you all right?' Zare asked, wiping his dirty face on his sleeve.

'No,' Beck said. 'I don't think I am.'

Zare looked out over the wreckage of the orchard and shook his head.

'I don't believe it,' he said.

'I know you don't,' Beck said, getting to his feet. 'That's the problem, Zare. Come with me – you haven't seen anything yet.'

He inclined his head and picked his way through the

equipment. Zare followed, trying not to think of what the orchard had looked like just a few months ago.

Beck stopped at the crest of the hill and Zare joined him. He gasped. Below them, the ground had been levelled, then ripped open. Machinery was everywhere – whining drills, massive construction droids, and repulsorlift haulers surrounded deep pits. Behind them were rows of prefabricated buildings, split by a road choked with speeder trucks. Miners in filthy jumpsuits were everywhere, hurrying between tasks. A massive crane lifted a load of rock from one of the mines, dropping it with a crash in the bed of a hauler. Dust billowed into the air and then the hauler started up, belching exhaust.

'This equipment is primitive stuff that should have been melted down before the Clone Wars,' Zare said. 'My parents have worked alongside mining installations before – they were nothing like this. They were pinpoint operations that left the surrounding land intact.'

'That would cost credits the Empire isn't willing to spend,' Beck said. 'It's like this for kilometres, you know – they're strip-mining the land, then leaving whatever's left to blow away in the wind. They don't even fill in the pits.'

Zare stared out at the mining camp, feeling numb.

'So enlighten me, Zare,' Beck said. 'Since Merei wouldn't come, you run the numbers for me. Explain to me why destroying Lothal will make life better everywhere else. Because this is a good thing, right? It must be, because the Empire you adore would never do anything wrong.'

Zare could only hang his head.

The long ride home through the cold night left Zare feeling stiff and tired. His parents were asleep, but Auntie Nags was still puttering around in the kitchen, hunting for non-existent particles of dust.

'Don't come in here, Zare Leonis – you're caked in filth,' she warned, photoreceptors yellow. 'What a disgrace! Where have you been?'

'Riding with Beck,' Zare said. 'I just wanted something hot to drink – maybe a cup of caf?'

'At this hour?' Auntie Nags chirped, hands on hips. 'You'd be awake all night, and you need your sleep. It's important that you be well-rested this week. Your sister's coming home for winter break, your application for the Academy isn't finished and needs to be transmitted, and of course there's the championship game.'

Zare sat down at the table, legs splayed, and stared at the floor. The Academy. He'd been sitting at this same table when Dhara got her acceptance message. He'd watched their mother enfold her in a hug, and their father blink back tears as he waited with a broad smile to offer his own congratulations.

Zare had been happy, too – but also jealous that he had to wait a year, twiddling his thumbs in some Outer Rim bantha school while Dhara got a head start on serving the Empire.

He didn't feel jealous now. All of a sudden the Academy felt like . . . like what, exactly?

Like a trap. That's what it feels like.

His parents thought the way to fix the Empire's mistakes was to serve it and show people a better way, but what if they'd been tricked? What if they'd all been tricked? What if the Empire really belonged to the faceless bureaucrats who'd signed the orders turning orchards into wastelands? What if it really belonged to bullies like Fhurek – bullies with Academy connections?

'How about some hot chocolate?' Auntie Nags asked. 'With tang bark, the way you like it.'

Zare looked up, momentarily puzzled, then realised the old nanny droid had been nattering on about the perils of caffeine at night for growing children.

'That . . . that would be great,' Zare said. 'Thank you, Auntie Nags.'

And then, to his horror, he felt his eyes well up and tears start to roll down his cheeks. He wiped them away, embarrassed, and saw the backs of his hands were covered in dirt from the wreckage of the orchardlands. He scrubbed futilely at the dirt for a moment, then gave up, sobbing.

'There, there,' Auntie Nags said, patting his shoulders, photoreceptors pulsing with soothing green light. 'There, there.'

Over the weekend AppSci had come down with a serious case of SaberCats fever. The hallways were festooned with green-and-white banners, students were wearing face paint, and Zare and his teammates couldn't get from one class to the next without running a gauntlet of high-fives and backslaps and fist bumps.

He should have been happy about all the attention, but it just made him feel slightly ill. He dreaded running into Hench or Frid, worried he wouldn't be able to keep his composure if they wanted to talk about the game that Fhurek didn't think they should play.

Somehow he managed to get through an entire day of classes without seeing either player. He didn't see them in the locker room, either, though Beck was there, grim and silent. The two of them put on their armour and headed for the grid, saying nothing, helmet straps dangling from their fingers.

Hench and Frid weren't on the grid, either. Now Zare was worried. It wasn't like either of them to be late.

On the sidelines, Coach Ramset was instructing Merei on the finer points of trap-kicks. Zare waved mechanically at the knots of cheering AppSci students who'd braved the cold to watch practice.

'Coach, where's the rest of the squad?' he asked.

'Not here,' Ramset muttered.

Zare looked over at Merei, who shrugged.

'Not here?' Zare asked, his stomach knotted with anxiety. 'Where are they?'

'You better ask the athletic director,' Ramset said.

Zare's cleats echoed in the hallway. He forced himself to think. Fhurek couldn't have ordered Ramset to simply cut Hench and Frid; the AppSci students and parents would have a fit about dropping two of the team's better players before the championship game. And something told Zare the athletic director wouldn't want to display his prejudices quite so obviously. But then what had he done?

Fhurek's office door retracted into the wall before Zare could buzz for entry; the athletic director had heard the sound of his cleats. One corner of Fhurek's mouth twitched, then swelled into a predatory smile.

'Ah, Leonis,' he said. 'I was just about to have Coach

Ramset send you up here. Too bad you didn't get a chance to congratulate your former teammates before they left.'

'*Former* teammates? Congratulate them for what?' Zare asked. He stood tentatively at the doorway.

'You haven't heard?' Fhurek asked, approaching Zare. 'Sina and Kelio have been transferred to the Technical Institute for Agricultural Research, effective immediately. The Institute may not have as good an academic reputation as AppSci, but it has some excellent programs – it's a great opportunity for them.'

Zare just stared at him.

'Fortunately, you and Coach Ramset have the week to work with whatever members of the practice squad you choose to take their places. Best of luck, Leonis – we're all cheering for you.'

And with that Fhurek stepped back into his office and left Zare staring at the closed door.

Coach Ramset was running tackling drills in the centre of the grid when Zare returned. Merei saw Zare first and intercepted him on the sidelines.

'Fhurek arranged for them to be transferred,' Zare said before she asked.

'That dirty conduit worm. So are we promoting Windrider and Rennet from the practice squad?'

'What? Who cares? We're not going to play,' Zare said as he stomped onto the grid. 'Coach? I need to talk to the team for a minute. Players only.'

Ramset saw the anger on Zare's face and nodded, retreating to the sidelines.

'Huddle up,' Zare said, and then told them what had happened. Kord Plandin, the sleepy-eyed keeper, said a word that would have had him running laps if Coach Ramset had heard it. Beck stared into space, hands on his hips. The other players kicked at the grass, eyes down.

'So what are we gonna do?' Bennis asked.

'Boycott the title game,' Zare said. 'I'm sorry, Windrider and Rennet – none of this is your fault. But Frid and Hench are our teammates – Fhurek doesn't just get to send them away. If he wants a title for AppSci, he can bring them back to play for it.'

'And if he won't?' Orzai Atropos asked. 'What do we do then?'

'Like I said, we don't play. Fhurek told me our title would be somehow tainted if we won with alien players. That's a bunch of poodoo – but it really would be tainted if we let him get away with this.'

He looked around at the SaberCats, but they weren't looking back. Their eyes were on the ground or their own equipment.

'I don't know, Zare,' Atropos said. 'I don't like this – it's a lowdown dirty thing to do. But what can we do? I mean, he's the athletic director – this is way bigger than us.'

'He's the athletic director, not the Emperor,' Zare said as his teammates turned away.

Ramset walked over from the sidelines, clapping his hands and talking about blocking drills. The other SaberCats put their helmets on, and Zare saw that several of them were grateful for their coach's interruption. He looked at them in disbelief, then shook his head and marched off the grid.

'Zare!'

Merei was jogging to catch up with him.

'I can't believe it,' Zare fumed. 'They're just going to let this happen? They don't even care!'

'Of course they do. They just don't think they can do anything about it.'

'Then they're wrong. But they don't care about that, either, the cowards.'

Merei shook her head. 'They're not cowards. That's not fair and you know it. You don't get what this means to them, Zare.'

'I don't?' Zare turned to stare at Merei, who had to back-pedal to avoid colliding with him. 'Then explain it to me. I know you will anyway.'

'I will if you'll *listen*,' Merei said. 'You're headed for a different life, Zare – highly paid agricultural scientist at least, maybe an Imperial officer. I am, too – it's stupid to pretend otherwise. But most of them will be lucky to get jobs as field technicians for one of the ministries here on Lothal. Whatever happens in the title game, you'll be at the Academy a year from now, probably already starting officer training. But they'll be in trade school – and being academy-league champs could make a big difference in what school they get into, and in their lives after that.'

'And that's not true of Frid and Hench, too?'

'I didn't say that. But you can't help Frid and Hench.'

Zare kicked at the grass. 'So I should just let Fhurek win, then,' he muttered.

'I didn't say that, either. But remember those guys back there on the grid are your teammates, too.'

The other SaberCats didn't say anything when Zare walked back onto the grid, helmet on. Neither did Coach Ramset; he just tossed him a grav-ball. The team worked through passing drills like nothing had happened, with Zare calling out routes for Hanc Windrider. Then they began practising blocking and carries, as poor Firmus

Rennet tried not to look nervous.

Zare never stopped being angry – the thought of Fhurek made him want to break something – but the routine did prove comforting. Afternoon practice was divided up into tasks that made sense, and that he could accomplish. Do a dozen carrying drills with Beck and Rennet. Now execute twenty passes to Windrider and Bennis. Then block for Merei on ten trap-kicks and ten kick-scores. Then drop back to assist Atropos, Umber, and Plandin on a dozen defensive routes.

Midweek brought an unseasonably warm day, and Zare emerged from the locker room after practice to find Merei waiting for him, datapad tucked under one arm.

'I've been scouting Kothal,' she said.

'And?'

'And we can beat them,' Merei said.

'You seem awfully confident,' Zare said. 'Roughnecks is a good name for Kothal. Don't they have that beast of a fullback? Farm boy, even bigger than Beck?'

'Yep – his name's Targol.'

'That's right. And their alien wing striker – the Aqualish – has both speed and size.'

'Horst Prajil.'

'I didn't know his name. I guess Kothal's athletic

director thinks aliens are good enough to play for him. So when do we get to the part where you're confident?'

'Right now,' Merei said, tapping at her datapad. 'Look at their centre striker. I've put footage of several plays together.'

'Let's go sit in the stands,' Zare said. 'If I don't sit down I might fall down.'

It was almost dark. The eastern sky was black, decorated with stars and the lights of starships in orbit, while overhead the sky was purple, shading to dark blue and then green in the west, the last sign of the departed sun. Zare settled himself in the stands and Merei sat beside him, turning towards him to share her datapad.

'These are all carry plays to Targol,' Zare said after they watched for a minute. 'Are you trying to depress me?'

'No. Pay attention to the centre striker. Now watch the plays again.'

Zare frowned down at the bright light of Merei's screen, hunting for whatever had her so excited and trying not to think of the pressure of her hip against his.

'Wait, go back,' he said. 'When he's going to Targol he holds the ball against his right thigh. Probably to get the ball to him a little earlier.'

Merei grinned.

'And he does it every time? Because you've taught me not to trust my eyes unless they're looking at a maths equation.'

'You're not funny,' Merei said, wrinkling her nose at him. She smiled at him, then looked down quickly. 'No, he doesn't do it every time, but pretty much,' she said. 'Here. I put together footage of some random plays. Watch and see if you can predict which ones are going to be carries to Targol.'

Zare got six out of seven.

'Nice work,' he said, and Merei gave a little bow. Zare thought it over. If he could spot the centre striker positioning the ball, a quick yell would warn the SaberCat defenders to break towards that side and bring up the wing defenders. That would make it harder for Targol to rack up big advances, and tire him out more quickly.

'But we still don't have Frid and Hench,' Zare said. 'Windrider and Rennet have been OK, but they were on the practice squad for a reason.'

'I know,' Merei said. 'But we're better than Kothal at most other positions. If we can slow Targol down, he'll tire by the third period. We can beat these guys – I know it.'

Zare nodded, then noticed Merei biting her lip.

'There's something else, isn't there?'

'Fhurek,' she said. 'Turns out he doesn't just have Academy connections – he also hangs out with some shady company. He's put a pretty big bet on us in the title game. Two thousand credits that we'll win by at least eight points.'

'How do you know that?'

Merei turned off her datapad and looked at Zare for a long moment. 'I might have gained access to his personal messages,' she said.

'You might have?'

'Mm-hmm. He made the bet after an argument with a friend at the transportation ministry, about whether mixed-species teams suffer from poor morale. It's nasty stuff.'

Zare nodded, then smiled.

'So we need to win, but only by six.'

'That's what I was thinking,' Merei said quietly.

'Isn't what you did illegal?'

'Highly. Are you going to report me?'

Zare grinned. 'Are you kidding?' he asked. 'I could kiss you.'

And a moment later, he did.

He drew back after a moment, thinking that her hair smelled like jogan blossoms.

Merei smiled at him. 'I've been wondering for a long time what that would be like,' she said.

'And?'

She put her hand behind his head and pulled him closer.

'And shhh,' she said.

With Dhara's return for winter break, Zare's spirits lifted and even Auntie Nags's photoreceptors seemed locked on green. On the night of Zare's fifteenth birthday, the Leonises sat over dinner into the night, laughing over stories from Hosk Station and Moorja and Viamarr and other worlds they'd half forgotten. His sister's easy smile and warm eyes let Zare forget Fhurek, and the orchardlands, and the feeling that everything he had relied on was untrustworthy and dangerous.

Then Auntie Nags brought out a decorated glaze cake and his father told him that since he was now fifteen, it was time to get his datapad and transmit his application to the Imperial Academy.

Zare forced himself to smile as his family applauded, then headed for his room, grateful that none of them could see his face. He picked up his datapad and took it back to the kitchen table, thumbing the activator.

His application was almost completely filled out. Both of his parents had checked over the form at least three times for the smallest mistake.

'Dhara, I believe we'll need you first,' Leo said,

handing the datapad to his daughter with a flourish.

'Let me see,' Dhara said, peering at the screen and pretending to be solemn. '"I, Dhara Leonis, of Capital City, Lothal, do hereby certify that Zare Leonis is personally known to me and of good moral character." Well, I suppose that's true if you don't count a history of stealing sweet-sand cookies and sassing poor Auntie Nags. But perhaps we should get Merei Spanjaf's opinion?'

Zare rolled his eyes. Dhara grinned at Zare and their parents, then looked back down at the datapad.

'Uh-oh, Zare – this next part's more problematic,' she said. '"Applicant Zare Leonis has no history of insurrection, rebellion, or rendering aid to the enemies of the New Order, is fit in every way to serve the First Galactic Empire, and enters into this agreement legally and voluntarily."'

She looked up at Zare, smiling . . . and then her smile faded when she saw his face.

Zare felt his cheeks flush.

'What?' Leo asked. He'd missed the look that had passed between his children, and was still smiling. 'I didn't twist the boy's arm!'

Zare grinned desperately, wondering what his sister had seen. She hurriedly smiled, too, then looked back down at the datapad.

'OK, Dad says there was no arm-twisting, so we can move on,' she said. 'Let's see. "I have been personally acquainted with Zare Leonis for fifteen years and zero days in the following capacity: sister." You didn't write "inspiration," or even "tormenter," but we'll let it slide. Everything looks in order. Anything I missed, Zare?'

Zare was aware of her eyes on him. What would happen if he said nothing? The moment would be funny at first. Then the delay would turn awkward. His father would tell him to hurry, Auntie Nags's photoreceptors would turn yellow, and his mother would become quiet and still, sensing that something was wrong.

Which Dhara already knew.

'Let's do this,' he said.

'All right then,' Dhara said. She pressed her thumb on the datapad's screen and it flickered, verifying her identity. She scrolled to the bottom of the application and nodded. 'All done, Zare. You just need to hit "transmit."'

Zare reached for the datapad, forcing himself to meet his sister's gaze. The future was clouded, but he couldn't bear the idea of bringing grief and strife to his own family's kitchen table.

He hit "transmit" and tried to smile.

Dhara waited, as Zare had known she would, until their parents had gone to bed and Auntie Nags and her occasionally overactive auditory sensors were busy in the kitchen. Then she inclined her head and he obediently followed her into her bedroom. The bed was immaculately made – blanket folded and creased, pillow perfectly straight.

'Academy training,' Dhara said, seeing him studying the bed. 'I remade it the second I got home, before it could bother me. Inspections and demerits get in your head.'

'I'm not looking forward to that,' Zare said. Auntie Nags complained every morning that his own bed looked like an ion storm had hit it.

'You want to tell me what happened back there?' Dhara asked.

Zare sighed, looking out the window at the lights of the city. 'How do you *always* know? It's annoying, sis.'

'Like the form said, I've been personally acquainted with you for fifteen years and zero days. Now quit stalling and talk to me.'

Zare started to sit down on his sister's bed, then looked at the perfect sheets and reconsidered, settling into the chair at her desk instead. And then it all came pouring out of him – the orchardlands and how they'd been wrecked, Fhurek and what he'd done to Frid and Hench. He left out Beck misleading the stormtroopers, and Merei's accessing Fhurek's messages, but he told his sister everything else, head either buried in his hands or thrown back to stare at the ceiling. When he was done he felt empty and exhausted.

'Well,' his sister said quietly. 'You've had quite a winter.'

Zare just nodded.

'And now you're wondering if we're wrong about the Empire.'

Zare hesitated, then nodded again.

'There's no reason for what they're doing in the orchardlands,' he said. 'They're destroying everything – nothing will ever grow there again. Is that why we came to Lothal, Dhara? To help them do that? Remember the day we arrived? Remember how good the air smelled, and how it felt to see blue skies instead of a durasteel ceiling? Now it's all being ruined.'

'You're reading a lot into one mining operation,' Dhara said. 'This is a big planet, with room for mining and industry as well as farms. I understand why your friend Beck is upset – I would be, too. But should the Empire let valuable ore or crystals or whatever they found out there go to waste because someone's grandfather picked that spot to plant jogan-fruit? Does that really make sense?'

'Maybe not,' Zare said. 'But they don't need to wreck whole kilometres to extract ore. They're using machinery out there that the Trade Federation would have been embarrassed to use.'

Dhara frowned. 'Look, Zare,' she said, voice low. 'The Empire isn't a machine. It's made up of people. Most of the ones I've met are pretty great – they want to make the galaxy a better place. But a few of them aren't so great. They make mistakes – bad ones, sometimes, like what happened to your friend's old farm. And some of them are bullies, or worse – like your athletic director. They're the kind of people who give the Empire a bad name. The way I see it, it's up to the rest of us to find them and stop them from doing more harm.'

'Agreed,' Zare said.

'Good,' Dhara said. 'But that kind of change only happens from within.'

'Be patient, in other words. Just like everybody else says.'

'Yes,' Dhara said. 'But you also need to be careful. That goes for your friend Beck, too.'

'What are you saying, Dhara?' Zare asked, trying to keep the fear out of his voice.

His sister saw his nervousness and smiled. 'Relax, Zare – people don't go to jail because they disagree with the way a mine's being run. That's not the way the Empire works. But you do need to remember where the Empire came from – it rose from the ashes of a government that was so consumed by conflict and jealousy and greed that it couldn't function, and from a terrible war in which billions died. The Empire won't let the galaxy go back to that – here on Lothal or anywhere else. That's why it takes safety and security so seriously.'

'Well, sure,' Zare said. 'I understand that.'

'Then you also understand the importance of not getting mixed up in something that could make you look like a threat to that security – particularly since you're a candidate for the Academy,' Dhara said. 'You're so close, little brother – just get through a few more months and everything will change. I promise.'

'SABERCATS! HUDDLE UP!'

The AppSci students nearest to the SaberCats' bench heard Zare's call and began to yell and wave their green-and-white banners. Zare swatted at a cam droid that flew too close and reached out his arm to draw Merei into the circle of their teammates, finding Beck with his other hand. He brought the two of them close and looked around the little group. Hanc Windrider was wide-eyed and pale and Zare smacked his helmet.

'So this is the championship game,' Zare said. 'Wow! There sure are a lot of people yelling, and a ton of cam droids.'

He let the moment linger, looking at each of the SaberCats in turn, trying to assess who was ready and whose nerves were threatening to get the better of them.

'But guess what – the grid's the same length it was yesterday,' he said. 'The ball's the same size. The clock will count down the same way it always does. Remember the plays, listen to me, and give it everything you've got. If you do that, the rest will take care of itself. You got that?'

Heads nodded.

'Not good enough. YOU GOT THAT, SABERCATS?'

This time his teammates roared that they did.

'That's better. Now Coach wants to say a few words.'

Ramset stepped into the circle, blinking his red eyes. 'You've played like champions all year,' he said simply. 'Now go make it official.'

The SaberCats jogged to the centre of the grid, accompanied by cheers from their home fans. They lined up opposite the Kothal players, wearing their orange-and-grey visitors' uniforms. Both squads stood at attention for the Imperial anthem, helmets under their arms, then shook hands.

'Good luck,' Zare told the Kothal centre striker. The other boy looked at him quizzically.

'Well, kind of,' Zare added, and the Kothal player nodded and smiled.

AppSci won the opening roll of the chance-cube and started with the ball.

'March!' Zare yelled over the cheering crowd, which included his parents and sister. Fhurek was up there, too, he knew; Merei had made sure he found out about the Kothal centre striker's habit, and told Zare that the athletic director had doubled his bet on the SaberCats to win by eight or more.

But Zare immediately had other problems than trying to foil Fhurek's schemes. Targol was indeed huge: the Kothal fullback wrapped up Zare on the first play, a blown carry to Rennet, and slammed him to the turf, forcing the air out of his lungs.

'Gonna be a long day,' the boy said with a grin.

'Keep bringing it,' Zare managed through gritted teeth, patting his opponent's helmet.

AppSci marched slowly down the grid, but the Roughnecks spoilt passes to Bennis and Windrider in the sixth octet, and on third drive Zare signalled for Merei. Her kick sailed cleanly through the circle to give AppSci a 2–0 lead.

It was the Roughnecks' turn, and they started with a mix of weak-side carries and passes, with Horst Prajil leaping high above Umber for a graceful catch on third drive. On the next play, Zare saw the centre striker set up with the ball against his right thigh.

'OMEGA! OMEGA! OMEGA!' he yelled, sliding left behind AppSci's fullbacks.

Targol shrugged off Firmus Rennet's tackle, but Zare and Beck were right behind him and brought down the hulking Kothal player with only a short gain. They sniffed out the next carry to Targol as well, and Kothal had to settle for a kick-score and a 2–2 tie. But two series later, Targol smashed Firmus aside and collided with Beck, who stumbled and fell. Before Zare could get his arms around the big Kothal fullback, he whirled and tossed a lateral pass to Prajil, who'd faked out Umber and dropped back to put himself in perfect position. Zare and Beck turned to each other in disgust as Prajil steamed down the grid, slammed the ball past Plandin's fingertips, and gave Kothal a 6–2 lead.

'Stang,' Beck told Zare and Firmus as the Kothal players whooped it up in the scoring circle. 'That guy's a one-man wrecking crew.'

'I know – but he's only one man. Stick to the plan.'

Merei's kick-score cut Kothal's lead to 6-4 as the first triad ended. In the second triad, the Roughnecks leant hard on Targol, who rumbled through octet after octet for a touch-score and a 10-4 lead.

'We know when they're giving the ball to him but he's still scoring,' Beck said.

'We're making him earn every carry,' Zare said. 'He'll get tired.'

'I hope it's soon,' Beck replied. 'Because I already am.'

'After we win you'll have all spring to rest.'

Merei and the Kothal kicker alternated kick-scores, making the score 12-6 in Kothal's favor. With time ticking down in the second triad, the Roughnecks went back to Targol and marched down the grid, with the big fullback harried on every carry by multiple SaberCats. Responding to the SaberCats' coverage, Kothal's centre striker tossed a short pass to Targol instead of handing off for a carry. Targol caught the ball and rumbled into the scoring circle. He smashed Plandin aside, raising the ball above his head and aiming at the goal.

Zare turned away in disgust.

'No goal!' yelled the referee.

Zare turned back, shocked. The big fullback's jump had come up short. He'd missed the touch-score.

Beck nodded at Zare. 'He's getting tired.'

Zare smiled and smacked the side of Beck's helmet.

'Twenty minutes left,' he said. 'We can do this. Concentrate on Targol's side. Let's make him more tired.'

The SaberCats went to work on the strong side of the Roughnecks' defence, with Zare mixing up carries to Firmus with passes to Windrider. Hanc missed an easy catch in the sixth octet and AppSci had to settle for a kick-score, but Targol was walking slowly now, breathing hard and stopping after each play to put his hands on his knees. The SaberCats kept Kothal from scoring on the next series and recovered the Roughnecks' trap-kick in the second octet.

'It's twelve–eight,' Zare reminded his teammates. 'A touch-score ties it.'

The SaberCats had to settle for another kick-score instead, but now they were within two – and they quickly regained the ball as Kothal's offence sputtered. As Zare walked to the line the crowd began to cheer, sensing the momentum swinging AppSci's way.

'March!' Zare said.

Beck slammed through the Kothal defenders for a

long run that took AppSci into the third octet. Then Zare went to work, forcing Targol to defend against repeated carries to his left, his right, and straight at him. Trying to help their tiring fullback, the Roughnecks doubled the coverage on Targol's side – which allowed Zare to hit Bennis for a pass that took AppSci into the eighth octet and let the SaberCats take aim at the scoring circle. Two plays later, Beck lowered his shoulder, stomped past the Kothal centre striker, and handed the ball off to Windrider, who flung it behind his head through the goal for a 14–12 AppSci lead.

'Nothing fancy,' Zare chided Hanc, but they were both grinning.

On Kothal's first play after the score, the centre striker handed off to Targol, who shoved Firmus aside. But Beck covered the hole in the AppSci defence and hit Targol in the midsection. As the crowd gasped, the ball popped into the air, then seemed to hang suspended under the lights for an impossibly long moment.

Zare felt like he was floating. He watched his hands come up and saw the ball come down into them. He juggled it for a moment, then squeezed it to his side. Targol reached up for Zare, eyes wide, Beck sprawled across his legs. The Kothal player got his fingers on Zare's knee, but then Zare twisted away from him. He lowered his head and chugged down the field, dodged the Kothal defenders, and heaved the ball through the goal, then put his hands on his knees, gasping. A moment later his teammates arrived, happily pounding him on the back and helmet. He fended them off and lifted his head, looking first to the sidelines where Merei stood beaming, then up into the stands where Dhara was jumping up and down, howling with glee.

AppSci 18, Kothal 12. Six minutes to go. Then Kothal's centre striker sent up a wobbly pass that Umber intercepted, giving the ball back to AppSci. Zare alternated between carries to Beck and Firmus, with both players pushing through the exhausted Kothal defence, and Hanc Windrider scored a touch-score with four minutes left to put AppSci up by ten.

The students cheered wildly, but Zare caught Merei's eye on the sidelines. She nodded, eyes flicking momentarily to the stands behind her, and Zare knew she was thinking the same thing he was: Fhurek must be already counting his credits.

Kothal used up a minute on a drive that stalled in the middle of the grid, and AppSci got the ball in the second octet. Zare flipped a short pass to Windrider and wound up entangled with Prajil as the play ended. Unable to help himself, he looked into the stands and saw Fhurek grinning, slapping hands with a gaggle of white-haired alumni wearing fancy tunics and green-and-white AppSci scarves.

'I'm sending all but one striker hard right,' Zare said to Prajil. 'Be a shame if we got our signals tangled and I missed a pass hard left.'

'You trying to insult us?' the Aqualish rumbled, his small black eyes hard with anger. 'We don't need your charity.'

'It's no gift – I've got my reasons,' Zare said.

Prajil shook his head, tusks parting slightly in anger. Zare called the play, then looked hard left to Windrider, who was shadowed by a defender in orange and grey. He fired the ball that way, aiming short, and watched as the Kothal player darted in front of Hanc and caught the ball, then charged back down the grid. Zare turned to chase him down, then was knocked sprawling – Prajil had run back from his position to receive a lateral pass. Through the legs of the other players, Zare watched as Prajil made the touch-score, then tried not to smile.

AppSci twenty-two, Kothal sixteen. Tough luck, Fhurek.

AppSci took the ball back at centre grid. Zare looked at the clock. There were two minutes left – plenty of time to go down the grid against the Kothal defence and score again.

'Gamma offence,' Zare said, forcing himself not to look in Fhurek's direction.

'We're not going for another score?' Firmus Rennet asked.

'We're up by six with two minutes to go,' Zare said. 'Just burn the rest of the clock and don't drop the ball – no need to rub it in their faces.'

Well, except one face, he thought.

The SaberCats moved steadily but methodically and found themselves in the sixth octet with the clock stopped and five seconds to go. They had one play left. Unable to resist, Zare looked over to the sidelines, where Merei stood. She had her helmet on the bench beside her, knowing she wouldn't be asked to kick.

Zare smiled, then walked to the line.

'March!' he yelled.

He dropped back, glanced at the clock, then hugged the ball to his chest and knelt down in the grass as time expired. The AppSci stands exploded in delirium and the students began to pour onto the field, hands raised. Zare stood, turned, and Beck plowed into him, lifting him in his arms as his other teammates converged from all sides. He raised the ball triumphantly over his head. The SaberCats had won by six and were league

champions.

PART 3:
SPRING

A week after the SaberCats celebrated their championship win, Zare walked down the main hallway of AppSci, returning the congratulations of his fellow students with brief nods. He was too angry to do more than that.

He found Coach Ramset in his cramped office, one level below Fhurek's.

'Ah,' Ramset said, his face turning a deeper green. 'Zare.'

'Coach, why did I get all these demerits?' Zare asked, brandishing his datapad. '"Failure to keep sports equipment in proper condition"? "Failure to secure personal effects in locker room"? What's all this nonsense?'

'I meant to speak with you about these things,' Ramset muttered. 'Your helmet was, um, frequently dirty. Unacceptable, Zare.'

'My helmet was dirty? It's grav-ball!'

Ramset shrugged and his shoulders slumped.

'Fhurek made you do this, didn't he?' Zare asked.

The Duros coach didn't say anything.

'Never mind,' Zare said in disgust. 'Let him have his revenge – I don't care. Are you going to coach chin-bret this term? I'm trying to pick between that and something simpler – like maybe track and field.'

'I'm afraid the chin-bret squads are full,' Ramset said.

'How can that be? You haven't even held tryouts yet.'

Ramset didn't say anything.

'And track and field?' Zare asked.

Another helpless shrug.

'I understand,' Zare said, getting to his feet.

'Zare . . .'

He turned at the door. Ramset had finally lifted his head to meet Zare's eyes.

'You're a champion,' the coach said. 'Don't forget that.'

'Thanks,' Zare said. 'But now I need to get to class. Let's see if I can avoid any demerits for damaging the floor by walking on it.'

* * *

Zare was still steaming when he found Merei in the data lab and began angrily telling her what Fhurek had done. She looked around nervously and shushed him, taking his hand.

'You know Fhurek's gunning for you,' she said. 'Remember who his friends are. Don't make it worse.'

'I don't care,' Zare said.

'You need to not care in a different way,' Merei said. 'Just keep your head down. Get through this term, graduate, and then you never have to think about him again.'

'That's what everybody says,' he muttered.

'If everybody's saying it, maybe you need to start listening.'

'Maybe,' Zare said. 'But this isn't *right.*'

Merei didn't respond to that, which Zare supposed was the sensible thing to do.

'Never mind,' Zare grumbled. 'I keep thinking about the orchardlands. Beck was talking about them the other day – how the jogan trees would be blossoming now, if things were different.'

'I know,' Merei said. 'He told me that, too. He wanted to know if I could find anything else out about the Empire's plans for the site.'

'And did you?' Zare asked eagerly.

Merei sighed. 'Not you, too,' she said, tapping at her datapad. 'If there's some sort of master plan for mineral extraction, it's not public – and before you ask, no. I told Beck I won't risk it, and I meant it. I just finished my application for the Institute for Quantitative Studies – I'm not endangering that now.'

Zare raised his hands peaceably.

'Anyway, there's not a lot about the site that we didn't know in the fall,' Merei said. 'It's obvious that they're looking for crystals, probably for use in laser-targeting systems. Oh, and Governor Pryce approved a request of additional security for the site. Some of the local farmers have filed complaints about dust and pollution.'

'Good – somebody needs to,' Zare said.

He let his thoughts drift for a moment. Merei was undoubtedly right about keeping his head down; provoking the athletic director would just give him an opportunity for further mischief. He should keep a low profile and get to the Academy, where Fhurek would be just an unpleasant memory.

'Say, Merei – can you see Academy records?'

Merei blew her breath out, looking wary.

'Zare,' she said.

'Nothing secret – I promise.'

Merei shook her head. 'All right, I'll look – but I need

an anonymous connection,' she said, typing furiously. 'Hmmm. I can't get at sensitive internal stuff – you'd have to be within the network to do that – but there's basic information. What do you want to know?'

'What can you see about Ames Bunkle?'

Merei typed briefly, then nodded. 'Applied and accepted last spring, enrolled in autumn. That sound right?'

Zare nodded.

'He's been selected for stormtrooper training,' Merei read. 'His status is green.'

'Try my sister – Dhara Leonis.'

'You think I don't know your sister's name? Status green. Officer candidate. She's applied for an internship at Imperial headquarters. Status pending.'

'Try my name?'

Merei typed briefly.

'At least they know you exist – your application's pending. But . . . hmmm.'

'"Hmmm"? What does "hmmm" mean?'

'I don't know. There's a note in your file, marked ELIGIBILITY UNDER REVIEW. Let me see if I can find out more.'

Merei typed, then looked disgusted.

'What is it?' Zare demanded loud enough for the

other students in the data lab to look in their direction.

'Shhh,' she said. 'Calm down and I'll tell you. There's a letter in your file questioning your fitness for Imperial service.'

'Fhurek,' Zare said, his hands shaking with fury. 'He won't get away with this. When people understand what he's done, and why –'

'Zare,' Merei said, her voice low and urgent. 'Stop.'

'Stop what? Fhurek's trying to keep me out of the Academy! He's trying to wreck everything! Can't you ... can't you do something about it?'

'No,' Merei said. 'It's too dangerous. Please don't ask me to do that, Zare.'

'I know. I'm sorry – I shouldn't have asked. But this means I have to do something.'

'No, you don't,' Merei said. 'You *can't*. Stop and *think*, Zare. The letter went to the Academy administrators. When you make a big stink and the Academy asks how you discovered Fhurek's letter, what are you going to tell them? That you had your girlfriend go snooping during study hall?'

'It's their fault for having crummy security,' Zare said.

'I don't think that will make it OK.'

Zare opened his mouth, then closed it again.

'Exactly,' Merei said. 'Think about who your parents are, and who your sister is. One letter may not be enough to wreck your application, even if it's from Fhurek. But revealing that you've been rummaging around in Academy files? That really will ruin everything.'

Zare put his face in his hands. He wanted to scream. No, he wanted to march over to Fhurek's office and strangle the man. But Merei was right: he couldn't.

He couldn't do anything.

'How many times do I have to say it?' Merei asked. 'Just keep your head down. I promise I'll keep an eye on your file and let you know if anything changes.'

Zare nodded. 'Thank you, Merei.'

'You're welcome. Want to pay me back?'

'Of course.'

'Good.' She leant close to whisper in his ear, sneaking a kiss next to his eye. 'Then stay out of trouble. Please.'

Zare nodded. He tried to think of a joke he could make, but Merei's face was drawn and pale with worry.

'I'm worried about you,' she said. 'And Beck, too. I couldn't stand it if either of you got hurt.'

For a couple of months Zare managed to do nothing that would have made Auntie Nags nervous, let alone Merei. He focused on his schoolwork and then went home at the end of the day, feeling only a mild pang when he heard the teams working out at the athletic complex. When classmates asked why he wasn't playing a spring sport he offered vague excuses about being tired. As the weather warmed, he and Merei strolled through Capital City, crossing between the Old City and the new Imperial construction, of which there was more every week. And Dhara kept him informed about life at the Academy, from the physical assessments and personality tests to the combat drills and classroom instruction.

And every time he asked Merei about his application, she shook her head and said there was nothing to report. The letter was still in his file. His application was still pending.

The weather warmed and the grasslands began to sprout new growth, the shoots of green grass rapidly pushing aside the dry stalks of the previous year and forming a bright new carpet over the land. But the dust storms continued, and every time Zare heard Lothalites muttering about them, he thought of the orchardlands.

He might have managed to keep his promise to Merei if his mother hadn't sent him to the marketplace on an errand one night, and if he hadn't run into Beck there.

The two boys talked briefly about chin-bret and Fhurek. Then Zare looked around and leant closer.

'Have you been to the orchardlands recently?' he asked.

Beck looked wary. 'Why do you ask?'

'I was wondering if anything's changed.'

'Didn't you hear?' Beck asked. 'Governor Pryce explained how it was all a big mix-up. She was out there last night planting jogan seedlings with Grand Moff Tarkin himself.'

'Very funny. I'm serious.'

'Why do you care?' Beck asked, arms folded across his chest. 'You're not from Lothal. You and your family came here from the Core, or wherever it was, and when this planet's ruined and used up, you can just move on to another one. Just like the Empire will.'

'That's not the plan for Lothal and you know it,' Zare protested. 'I asked Merei about that, and so did you.'

'It's not the *official* plan for Lothal,' Beck said. 'But that doesn't mean anything. It's happened on other worlds, you know. Planet after planet, ruined and wrecked. You won't hear about it on Imperial HoloNet, but it's true. And now it's happening here.'

Beck stepped forwards, looking around to make sure nobody was listening.

'I have been out there,' he said. 'It's getting worse. The dust and water pollution are so bad that the farmers who didn't sell out can't work their fields. They can't make rent, so their farms are being seized and sold to the Empire. There are camps of displaced people now. Some of them filed a complaint with the governor, but she didn't even acknowledge it.'

'I didn't hear anything about that,' Zare said.

'Of course you didn't,' Beck said. 'You think Alston Kastle's going to lead the nightly vid with that bit of information?'

Zare hesitated, and Beck shook his head in disgust. 'Fine, don't believe me,' he said. 'Don't believe any of it. That will make it easier when you and your family pack up and go.'

'We aren't going anywhere,' Zare said. 'This is our home now. And I didn't say I don't believe you. I just want to see for myself.'

Beck narrowed his eyes and studied Zare for a long moment. Then he nodded. 'All right, then. We'll go tomorrow, after I finish practice. But keep it quiet. And come by my place – don't take your jumpspeeder.'

'Why not?'

'Because it's registered with the transportation ministry. And that means it can be tracked. We still have a bunch of old ones we used on the farm and never registered. We'll take two of them.'

'Isn't that – no, never mind. I'll see you tomorrow.'

The jumpspeeder that Beck lent to Zare was not only unregistered but souped up in a way that Zare suspected was illegal and knew was unsafe.

'There isn't much to do after harvest but tinker with speeders,' Beck said with a shrug as Zare admired the hot rod. 'Go easy on the throttle or she'll launch you over the horizon. And light on the starter or she'll flood.'

Feeling the power of the engine thrumming underneath him, Zare couldn't resist a grin. And flying down the road after Beck, he was able to briefly forget everything that had happened since that first trip west, when the year was so full of promise.

But the sight of the filthy river and the ravaged hills beyond it reminded Zare of what they were likely to find. Beck pulled off beside the old bridge, scowling down at the narrow crossing still marked off with flexi-tape.

'Wait for the hourly TIE patrol – it'll go by in a few minutes,' Beck said.

Zare nodded, staring down into the sluggish water. He heard the whine of the Imperial starfighters from upriver and watched as they passed overhead, climbing slightly and vanishing over the hills. Neither boy waved.

They crossed the new bridge downriver, then drove slowly up the hill. A new road intersected the main route where the old turn-off had been, following the path that had once led past the Ollets' house and up to the orchards. Beck's repulsorlifts sent little whirlwinds of dust into the air and Zare wiped at his face, conscious of the noise of his jumpspeeder's engine.

The road turned south below the crest of the hill, now crowned by a fence. The two boys rode their jumpspeeders along it, climbing the treeless ridge. They passed a huge rock that had been sheared in two, then followed the fence west for another half kilometre or so. There it turned north again, and on the other side of the road there were jogan orchards.

Zare felt a surge of hope when he saw the trees, but Beck had expected that reaction and shook his head.

'No one will ever eat them – something leaked into the groundwater, some kind of chemical used for breaking up rock,' he said. 'The Empire condemned this farm last week and made the workers move.'

'Where did they go?'

Beck stopped his jumpspeeder and began walking it through the orchard, away from the road. 'They went up here, with everybody else,' he said. 'We need to be quiet.'

They emerged from the abandoned orchard into an empty field that had been turned into a camp. Zare saw everything from modular housing and crisp tents to ramshackle little houses built of scrap metal and wood.

But there were no people around.

'Where is everybody?' he asked.

'Shhh,' Beck said, and then Zare heard it – a low buzz of voices from somewhere ahead. Then he heard another voice, amplified by a loudspeaker.

The two boys walked their jumpspeeders behind an old freight container and peered around it. Beyond another row of tents, a crowd of men and women had assembled and were listening to a bearded man with a loudspeaker.

'Farmers,' Beck said. 'They're local – I know some of them.'

'No, the governor hasn't responded to our complaint,' the leader said. 'But I'm told an Imperial representative is on his way to receive our petition.'

The farmers buzzed excitedly about this news.

'Now listen, please,' the leader said. 'Treat this representative with respect. No violence and no angry words. We've drawn up a list of people who will make statements in order, and we're going to stick to that list. We are Imperial citizens – we need to act like it, not like some rabble.'

Zare heard another sound now – the whine of repulsorlifts. As he and Beck watched, a troop transport advanced along the road from the other side of the camp.

The farmers stepped back from the gleaming craft, which drifted to a stop a few metres from their leader. Zare heard thumping in the west, and a pair of AT-DPs appeared, flanking an open-topped troop carrier. The stilt-legged walkers halted behind the gathering. Stormtroopers emerged from the troop carrier, forming a loose ring around the farmers. They had their blasters in their holsters.

The passenger door of the transport rose and an Imperial officer stepped out, wearing a crisp uniform.

'It's Lieutenant Roddance,' Zare said. 'My family knows him. C'mon, Beck!'

Before he could take two steps, Beck grabbed him by the shoulder and dragged him back behind the container, as if Zare were an enemy fullback trying to cross into the next octet.

'Are you crazy?' he demanded.

'Let's show them some support!' Zare said.

Beck shook his head urgently. Frustrated, Zare watched as the leader nodded at Roddance and raised his loudspeaker so the crowd could hear him. But before he could speak, Roddance raised his hand to stop him. Then the Imperial officer lifted a comlink to his lips, his voice emerging from the troop transport's speakers.

'This is an illegal assembly that violates security

protocols,' he said. 'On behalf of Governor Pryce, I order you to disperse.'

The bearded farmer looked at Roddance in surprise, then spoke into his loudspeaker.

'Our gathering is no threat to anyone,' he said. 'By Imperial law we have the right to petition the governor. If you won't bring our complaint to her, we will do so ourselves.'

'I am the law here,' Roddance said. 'Your complaint is denied. Disperse at once.'

The bearded farmer nodded at the people around him. In silent protest, they sat down in ones and twos until only Roddance and the stormtroopers were standing.

Roddance gestured at the stormtroopers and they waded into the crowd, dragging people up by their arms. Three troopers stepped forward, armour clattering, and drove the farmers' leader onto his face in the dirt.

'There's no need . . .' Zare said.

Then two stormtroopers raised their weapons, sending blue concentric circles of stun bolts into the crowd.

Someone screamed.

'We need to get out of here,' Beck said. 'Right now.'

He half dragged Zare to the parked jumpspeeders and started his bike. Zare was still staring in the direction of the camp in shock.

'Zare!' Beck said. 'We have to go! Follow me!'

Beck stomped on the throttle and his jumpspeeder shot away from the camp, with Zare following. As they crossed into the trees, Zare heard the thump of energy weapons behind them. He knew they weren't stun bolts.

Beck and Zare returned to Capital City by back roads that Beck knew, including a few that were little more than pathways through silent fields. When they got home, Beck told Zare to put the unregistered jumpspeeder in the Leonises' garage. Then he nodded and accelerated away towards his own home.

Zare returned to the apartment shortly before dinner, ignoring Auntie Nags's flurry of questions. He heard the familiar, comforting voice of Alston Kastle from the living room, reading the nightly news. He waved to his parents on his way down the hall to his bedroom.

'... report of trouble in the Westhills.'

Zare stopped, suddenly unable to breathe. He quietly returned to the living room, where his parents were watching Kastle on the holocaster.

'A spokesperson for Governor Pryce said the trouble started when insurgents destroyed mining equipment and attacked Imperial surveyors, requiring law-enforcement action to restore order. Governor Pryce's spokesman emphasised that the incident was an isolated disturbance and has been contained.'

Zare looked at the holocaster in horror. *Insurgents? Attacking people?* None of that had happened.

'I hope that law-enforcement action included a few good whacks with a rifle butt,' Leo grumbled.

'Leo – there's no need for that,' Tepha replied. 'But how disappointing to discover such lawlessness here on Lothal, too.'

Zare wanted to tell them that Kastle was lying – that none of it had happened that way. But he couldn't – he mustn't. He retreated to his bedroom. He would comm Dhara. She would know what to do.

But Dhara wasn't answering. It was too late for her to be in class. Zare waited for her to send back a quick message, some kind of reassurance that she was busy but would be in touch soon, but none came.

He reminded himself that the Academy instructors loved unexpected drills and other surprises. She'd probably been called away for another training exercise, with no time to tell her family.

Heck of a time for it, sis, Zare thought miserably. *I could really use your help.*

* * *

Zare's comlink beeped a couple of hours later. He answered it eagerly, hoping to hear his sister's voice.

But it was Merei.

'Congratulations!' she said.

'For what?' Zare asked, baffled.

'Your Academy status just changed to accepted.'

'It did?' He fumbled with his datapad, though he'd just checked his messages a minute ago, hoping Dhara might have responded.

'No message,' Zare said.

'You'll probably get one in a week or so,' Merei said. 'Try to act surprised.'

'But what about Fhurek's letter?'

'What about it? I told you it wouldn't matter, didn't I? This is what you wanted, Zare – I thought you'd be happy.'

'I – there's just a lot going on, that's all,' Zare said. 'Thanks for telling me, Merei.'

Dhara didn't contact her family by breakfast, but Zare's parents weren't concerned; they also assumed Dhara was engaged in some kind of training exercise. Zare's mother knew something else was bothering him and patted his hand, saying she was sure they'd learn he'd been admitted to the Academy in a couple of weeks.

Zare smiled back thinly, thinking of how many things he couldn't tell her.

That he'd already been accepted.

That the Empire was lying about what had happened in the orchardlands.

That the Empire had killed people who'd been protesting peacefully.

It was a lot to hide, and that morning it made him feel sick. He pushed aside his half-eaten breakfast, kissed his mother, gave his father a quick hug, and hurried off to school, where he tried to lose himself in lectures and studying. Exams were coming up soon, and though he knew he'd already been accepted to the Academy, he couldn't slack off; he'd heard horror stories about prospective cadets who'd ignored their studies, got bad grades, and received the worst kind of message over their datapads. Supposedly one kid had learned his acceptance had been rescinded while a tailor-droid was taking measurements for his uniform.

But Zare couldn't stop himself from hanging around until Beck was finished with chin-bret practice. His friend nodded at Zare as he exited the locker room.

'Any problems?' he asked in a low voice. 'Any sign you were followed?'

'No,' Zare said. 'But did you see the newscast?'

'I queued it up later. I was surprised they even mentioned it. They must have figured they couldn't just make that many people disappear.'

A couple of months ago, Zare thought, he would have objected angrily to the idea that the Empire would kill its own citizens. Now, he just nodded.

'And there's nothing we can do about it,' he said.

'That's where you're wrong,' Beck said. 'The Empire can be stopped – and I intend to help stop it. Because I know people who feel the same way.'

'People like what? Separatists? Some kind of underground here on Lothal?'

'Not yet, no,' Beck said. 'Or at least not that I know of. But if there isn't one, my friends and I will change that. Because somebody has to.'

'You're crazy,' Zare said. 'What you're talking about is impossible.'

'I'm not talking about bringing down the whole Empire,' Beck said. 'Just causing enough trouble so the Imperials will leave Lothal alone and go ruin some other planet. Let somebody else save the galaxy, Zare – I just want to save this little part of it.'

Zare looked at Beck, hoping this was the kind of youthful bravado Dhara loved to make fun of. But he could tell Beck wasn't kidding.

'Beck, don't,' he pleaded. 'The Empire's too powerful – no one can resist it. You're going to get yourself killed.'

'So I should wait for more places to be destroyed?' Beck demanded. 'For more people to disappear? Maybe I will get myself killed. At least my life will have had some meaning.'

A week later, they still hadn't heard from Dhara, and Zare's parents were alternating between annoyance at the Academy for scheduling an unreasonably long secret training exercise and the beginnings of actual worry.

Zare's comlink buzzed just as he was finishing his homework. It was Merei, and all he had to hear was the way she said his name to know it was bad.

'Just tell me,' he said, knowing she didn't want to.

'It's Dhara. Her status has changed.'

Zare fought to keep a wild surge of grief from spilling out of his chest and engulfing him – him, his parents, and everything else.

'Is she dead?' he managed to ask.

'I don't think so,' Merei said. 'Her status is now "inactive."'

'What does that mean?'

'I don't know. And there's something else. I was curious, so I looked through the other Academy records. Every other applicant for next year's class is marked "pending". Zare, you're the only one who's been accepted.'

'Despite Fhurek and the letter in my file,' Zare said. 'That doesn't make any sense.'

Just then the door chimed.

Commandant Aresko stood in the doorway, looking down at Auntie Nags. Zare's parents were standing by the kitchen table, looking at the Imperial officer in surprise – and sudden terror. Auntie Nags rolled back and forth, eyes yellow, searching for some programming that would tell her what to do.

'Please come in, Commandant,' Zare's mother said, offering him a chair with a shaky wave of her hand. 'Would you like something? Perhaps a tarine tea?'

Aresko walked into the apartment, but shook his head at the offer to sit. 'I'm afraid I have some bad news,' he said.

Zare's father guided his wife to a chair, then sat himself. Zare came to stand behind his parents. Aresko saw him and his eyes narrowed briefly. Then he nodded at Zare.

'Has something happened to our daughter?' Leo asked in a strangled voice.

'Unfortunately, yes,' Aresko said.

Zare braced himself, waiting for Merei to be wrong, to hear the words he dreaded.

'Cadet Leonis has . . . run off from the Academy,' Aresko said.

'What?' Zare demanded. 'That's impossible.'

Aresko's eyes jumped from his parents to him. 'I wish it were,' he said. 'She disappeared from camp during a training exercise in the Easthills. There was no sign of a struggle, and she took her backpack and supplies. We don't know why – she left no messages. That's one reason I came. Did Cadet Leonis indicate any unhappiness with her progress at the Academy?'

'Of course not,' Leo snapped. 'Dhara wanted to serve the Empire since she was a little girl. She was your star cadet, Commandant. She'd never do this. Never.'

'She certainly wouldn't do it without letting us know,' Tepha said.

Zare knew his parents were right. The last few months had shaken his belief in almost everything, but not in Dhara. Whatever had happened to her, she hadn't run away. The Empire was lying about that – as it had lied about so much else.

'Oh dear, oh dear,' Auntie Nags kept repeating as she made miserable circles in the kitchen.

'We're doing everything we can,' Aresko said. 'All security forces on Lothal have been directed to search for Cadet Leonis. And an alert has been placed in the Imperial customs and identification-processing databases, in case she's gone off-world. I can assure you that we'll let you know immediately if we hear anything.'

Aresko bowed his head slightly in farewell, eyes lingering on Zare. Then he was gone.

The next morning, a terse message informed Zare that he'd been accepted into the Imperial Academy. He stared at his datapad, then tossed it on the bed. Last summer all he'd wanted was the chance to join his sister and serve the Empire, and having to wait a year had seemed unbearable. Now the wait was finally over, but everything had changed. His faith in the Empire had been destroyed. And Dhara was gone.

Zare clicked on the message, then hit REPLY and stared at the datapad's blank screen, trying to will his fingers to work.

It's the right thing to do, he thought. *It's the only thing to do.*

He took a deep breath, then began to type.

In study hall the next day, Merei took the seat next to him, reached over, and squeezed his hand. He nodded gratefully at her.

'I saw your Academy status change this morning,' she said.

'To what?' he asked.

'Deferred,' she said. 'Did they try to contact you after you declined your acceptance? Not very many people give up a place in the Academy, you know.'

Zare shook his head. 'Nobody said a word. Is my sister's status any different?'

Merei shook her head. 'No. You know I'd tell you. What did your parents say when you told them you weren't going?'

'I didn't tell them yet,' Zare said. 'I couldn't. They're in shock.'

Merei nodded. 'So what are you going to do now?'

'Find out what really happened – what they did to her. And then I'm going to get her back. Will you help me?'

Merei looked at his face, at his blazing eyes. A flicker of fear crossed her face. But then it was gone, and she nodded.

'Of course I will,' she said.

When Beck saw Zare he didn't say anything, but he didn't have to. Despite Lothal's growing population, Capital City was still a small place where everyone soon knew everyone else's business. The big fullback picked up his pace so he could walk down the hall beside Zare, who found his heavy footsteps comforting.

They were almost to the geology classroom when Fhurek stepped around the corner into Zare's path.

'Can't say I'm surprised, Leonis,' he said in a low, poisonous voice. 'Apparently disloyalty runs in the family.'

Zare flung himself at Fhurek, teeth bared. It took Beck and three other students to pull him off the athletic director and drag him away.

'He's going to need a cold-pack for that eye,' Beck said with a small smile. 'Well, Zare, that's one demerit you can't argue with.'

Zare's parents had spent the first frantic weeks after Commandant Aresko's visit contacting everyone they knew at every Imperial ministry on Lothal, which made for a long list. Every minister, bureaucrat, and assistant they reached said the same thing: how sorry they were to hear about Dhara, how committed they were to helping the Leonises find her, and how they'd be in touch immediately if anything turned up.

But nothing did, and little by little, each of the Leonises found a way to resume lives that had been horribly rearranged.

Zare's father decided that the Empire was telling

the truth. Sometimes he was angry with himself for not recognising Dhara's distress, while other times he told Tepha and Zare confidently that he knew some Imperial minister somewhere was about to message them that Dhara had made contact and would soon be coming home.

Zare's mother was equally certain that the Empire was wrong – she could never quite bring herself to say "lying" – and became obsessed with the idea that Dhara hadn't been found because the Leonises hadn't contacted the right member of the vast Imperial bureaucracy, the one who had information that would end their search but didn't know its importance. That person was the missing piece of the puzzle tormenting their family, and she would find them.

As for Zare, he knew his mother was right and Dhara hadn't run away. But he couldn't bear to say what else he knew. It would have shattered his parents' last hopes, leaving them with nothing. He kept the secret locked inside, confiding only in Merei, and trudged grimly through the remainder of the school year.

It ended on a warm late-spring day with a joyless graduation ceremony. Merei had to remind him to fling his AppSci cap into the air.

PART 4:
SUMMER

The days grew longer and warmer until the summer heat became a thick blanket over Lothal, leaving the grasslands shimmering in the afternoon sun. There was no news of Dhara – nothing from the Imperial ministries Zare's parents checked with every day, and nothing from Merei's secret explorations of any database she could break into.

Dhara Leonis had simply vanished.

When Zare decided what he needed to do, Beck was gone, too; he didn't respond to his comlink or to messages sent to his datapad.

Beck's parents told Zare he was spending the month riding jumpspeeders around Lothal with his cousins as a break before starting work as a harvest supervisor in the fall. But Zare didn't believe that. He couldn't imagine Beck out for an extended joyride, not with everything that had happened.

In the marketplace one day, Zare caught sight of Frid Kelio, who let out a Rodian honk of surprise, then pushed his way through the crowd. Zare waited anxiously for his former SaberCat teammate, wondering if Frid knew why he'd been transferred out of AppSci, and if he blamed Zare.

But Frid gave Zare a friendly clout on the shoulder. 'Beck said you gave that lousy svaper Fhurek a black eye,' he said. 'Wish I could have seen that.'

'He had it coming,' Zare said. 'Have you talked to Beck recently?'

Frid looked away, his face mottled a darker green.

'Frid, I need to talk to him,' Zare said. 'Would you please just tell him to contact me?'

A couple of days later Zare was leaving his parents' apartment when someone called his name. He saw a figure standing in the shadows of the service alley. It was Beck, hooded and wearing goggles.

Zare looked around. The streets were empty; everyone had fled inside seeking shelter from the heat. He stepped into the alley.

'I figured I'd better come to you before you put up a public message on the HoloNet,' Beck said, looking annoyed. 'Well, you've found me. Now what do you want?'

'I know what you're doing,' Zare said. 'You're not out

sightseeing in the grasslands, or whatever it is you told your mother.'

'You're right, I'm not. So what?'

'I want to join you,' Zare said. 'I want to help. You heard about my sister. She didn't run away. She'd *never* do that to us. The Empire did something with her.'

'Your sister's dead, Zare,' Beck said.

Zare shook his head, biting his lip hard. 'I don't believe that.'

'Don't believe it, or *won't* believe it? She ran away, right? Just like the farmers in the Westhills. Their relatives were told they ran away, too, you know – a whole bunch of people who'd never travelled further than Capital City in their entire lives suddenly had an urge to see the galaxy. There's a lot of that going on these days.'

'Dhara's not dead,' Zare insisted. 'I don't know how I know, but I do.'

'Zare, I hope you're right – I mean that. But there are only a few of us working together so far. We can't search the galaxy for your sister.'

'I know,' Zare said. 'I just . . . you were right, Beck. They need to be stopped. And I want to help stop them.'

'And how are you going to do that, Zare? Are you willing to plant bombs? Shoot stormtroopers?'

Zare hesitated, then looked down at the ground.

'Didn't think so,' Beck said. 'Despite everything that's happened, you're still the little Imperial who thinks the galaxy is supposed to be a nice place. Leave me a message when you understand the stakes.'

And with that, he stalked off down the alleyway, leaving Zare alone.

The next day Merei commed Zare, frantic.

'It's Beck,' she said. 'I just got a message from him, thanking me for being a friend if he doesn't return. Did you find him? Do you know what he's doing?'

'No, but I can guess,' Zare said. 'I have to go.'

'I want to go with you.'

'No,' Zare said. 'That will just put more people in danger. And you can be more help by monitoring the security transmissions. Comm me if you hear anything.'

He clicked off his comlink, grabbed a pair of macro-binoculars, and raced out of the apartment, ignoring Auntie Nags's questions. Downstairs, he trundled Beck's unregistered jumpspeeder out of the garage where he'd left it. A few minutes later he was racing down the highway at an unsafe speed, the wind threatening to shove him off the powerful jumpspeeder.

Zare passed the narrow bridge, then took the larger

crossing over the river. The mine was still in operation on the ruined plain, which was pockmarked with deep pits and cloaked by blowing dust. The fences were gone, though. Zare guessed the Empire's brutal crackdown had eased its security concerns.

The orchards through which he and Beck had fled were still there, but as he neared the site of the camp Zare saw surveyor droids moving through the jogan trees, leaving broken branches in their path. He piloted the jumpspeeder through the dishevelled orchard, avoiding the droids, and found the farmers' camp was gone. The site was covered with heavy equipment: clearly the Empire's mining operations had now expanded west, to chew into new ground.

Zare raised his macrobinoculars and scanned the site, hoping for some sign of Beck. He saw nothing at first, but then a plain canvas satchel lying next to a jogan stump caught his eye.

Zare parked his jumpspeeder next to the bag and gingerly opened it.

It was full of detonators.

Then he was lying on his back, blinking at the spots in his vision, ears ringing. His first thought was that the detonators had gone off – but that couldn't be, because he'd be dead. He scrambled up on his elbows, trying to make sense of what he was seeing. The limbs of mining droids were scattered around, still sparking and twitching, and thick smoke rose from the centre of the mining site.

A landspeeder raced down the roadway leading back up into the hills. It was listing to one side; one of its repulsorlifts was damaged. Zare raised his macrobinoculars, trying to blink the spots out of his vision, and zoomed in on the speeder.

Beck was leaning out of the back window with a blaster in his hand. He fired a barrage of shots.

Behind the speeder came an Imperial troop transport.

Zare pressed himself into the dirt as the troop transport accelerated, chasing the speeder up into the orchards. Then he grabbed the satchel and slung it over his shoulder, leaping on the jumpspeeder. He started the engine, stomped on the throttle . . . and the engine died. He'd flooded it.

He forced himself to count to five, hands shaking with adrenaline, then started the speeder again, depressing the starter gently this time. The engine sputtered, then caught, and Zare shot off into the trees, spraying a fan of dirt behind him.

It was easy to follow the two vehicles: thick dust and churned-up dirt marked the path they had taken through the mining camp on what had once been the Ollets' land. Blinded by dust, Zare lost the path and had to cut hard left to avoid sailing into a deep pit, then swerve right to avoid a gang of miners and a construction droid. Coughing convulsively, he wiped a sleeve across his sweaty face and spat out dirt.

Auntie Nags is going to be furious, he thought, then laughed at himself.

They were past the mining camp now; he could see the speeder and the troop transport racing down the hillside towards the new bridge across the river. He was gaining on them. The speeder was listing badly, and Zare could feel the concussive thumps of the troop transport's dorsal cannons. Those were anti-vehicle guns, Zare remembered – much more powerful than the antipersonnel guns on either side of the vehicle's prow.

A crater bloomed to the right of the fleeing speeder, sending liquefied ferrocrete into the air. It rained down, smoke rising from the ground where it landed.

Zare measured the distance between the two vehicles, then looked from Beck's speeder to the bridge. His friend wasn't going to make it.

He pushed harder on the throttle and the jumpspeeder growled and lunged forwards. The jumpspeeder wobbled as he let go of the controls with one hand, hoping he wouldn't fall off.

He fumbled in the bag and emerged with a detonator in his fist.

The troop transport was directly ahead of him now. Zare thumbed the activator on the detonator. His comlink began to buzz. He glanced down at it, startled, then looked up and flung the detonator at the rear of the Imperial vehicle. It bounced in the roadway and disappeared under the transport.

A moment later flame erupted from underneath the transport, knocking it off the road in a crazy spin. Zare braked frantically, feet skidding on the roadway, trying to blink away sweat. The transport came to a halt, facing the way it had come, between Zare and the bridge.

He stomped on the throttle and cut hard to the left, racing along the polluted river. Out of the corner of his eye he saw Beck's speeder had crossed the new bridge and was shrinking to a dot in the distance.

An explosion ripped open the ground to the left of him, sending a shudder through his jumpspeeder. He ducked, then stomped on the throttle again, weaving back and forth to throw off the gunner's aim.

Another explosion punctured the roadway behind him, close enough that he could feel the heat on his back. He tried to think of a way to evade the transport and double back to the bridge, but it was hopeless. He was going to be caught or killed.

The bridge!

Zare looked to his right, eyes tracing the murky river, and found the narrow old bridge ahead of him. He cut left, then back to the right, then braked hard, one foot skidding along the ground. The troop transport shot past him, its gunner struggling to reorient the topside cannons as Zare aligned the jumpspeeder with the old bridge and stomped on the throttle.

The flexi-tape was a thin orange line across his path. Zare wondered how tough it was: would it knock him off the jumpspeeder, or cut him in two? He hit it with his chest and it stretched, then parted with a pop. A moment later he burst through the second length of tape, leaving the ends fluttering behind him.

Zare risked a look over his shoulder and saw the transport come to a stop on the far side of the bridge it was too wide to cross. Before the gunner thought to fire, Zare mashed the throttle down again and streaked down the highway through the fields, fleeing for Capital City.

It was Merei who had commed him, to warn him of a security alert in the area of the orchardlands.

Zare woke up repeatedly that night, waiting for her to comm him again, this time with worse news . . . or for stormtroopers to arrive at the door. Would they have the satchel he'd thrown away a few kilometres from the bridge? Ask about the unregistered jumpspeeder they'd tracked to the Leonis's garage? Or would they simply show up with Beck, already wearing binders?

But no one came. And no one commed him until Beck did the next morning.

'Meet me at the grav-ball grid,' he said, then hung up.

Zare rode his own jumpspeeder to AppSci, mind screaming that this was a trap. And when he saw Merei parking her own jumpspeeder, he could barely breathe.

'I'm so glad you're all right,' she said, rushing to embrace him. 'Beck commed me, too. Do you know what's going on?'

No stormtroopers awaited them on the grid. There was just Beck, standing in the centre of the AppSci logo with his head down.

'The Empire identified our speeder,' he said simply. 'They're searching for the occupants now.'

'Oh, no,' Merei said. 'Beck, you have to hide! Get out of sight!'

'That's what I'm going to do. Has anyone contacted you?'

'No,' Zare said. 'Maybe they didn't get a good look at you.'

Beck just shook his head. 'Some of the others have already stopped responding to messages. It's only a matter of time before they find me, too.'

'Beck –' Zare began.

'Listen to me, you two – this will have to be a short conversation. I was unfair to you the other day, Zare. You do understand the stakes. But you were right about the Empire. You both were. It's too powerful to take on openly. What we did was a mistake.'

'You don't mean that,' Zare said.

'I don't mean we shouldn't fight,' Beck said. 'It's just that the time isn't right yet. The Empire will crush any open resistance. You were lucky to escape, Zare. But you won't get that lucky again. And, Merei . . . you've got to be careful. Security is getting better all the time. They'll detect you snooping, and trace it back to you.'

'And when will the time be right?' Zare asked.

'Soon,' Beck said. 'The more the Empire tightens its grip, the more people will feel the squeeze – and realise it's fight back or be crushed. A real resistance will emerge. And when it does, they'll need people on the inside, who can help them.'

'People who have the Empire's playbook,' Merei said.

'Yes,' Beck said, looking at Zare. Then his eyes turned to Merei. 'Along with people who can scout the other team.'

'You think I should go to the Academy after all,' Zare said.

'If you really want to help, yes.'

'That's crazy,' Merei said. 'Zare's sister disappeared because she went to the Academy, remember?'

'I know,' Beck said. 'But if there's an answer to what happened to your sister, you'll find it in there, not out here.'

'It doesn't matter, because I already told them no,' Zare said. 'They'll never take me back now.'

'That's not true,' Merei said quietly, almost unwillingly. 'They will take you back. Remember how your status changed when your sister's did? How you were accepted before anyone else was, despite Fhurek's letter? They want you, Zare. They want you there.'

Beck nodded.

'You guys have always been a good team,' he said. 'You'll figure it out. And now I really do have to go. I doubt we'll see each other again. But you've been good friends. I'm sorry I didn't always realise that. But I won't forget it now.'

When Zare returned home his mother was at the kitchen table, staring down into a bowl of fruit, while his father had gone to the ministry to catch up on reports.

Zare swallowed nervously, then turned to

Auntie Nags.

'Auntie Nags, I need you to shut down,' he said. 'Mum and I are going to have a private conversation.'

The nanny droid's photoreceptors flared red as Zare's mother looked up, surprised.

'Zare Leonis,' Auntie Nags said. 'I was programmed to be discreet.'

'And I've learnt to be cautious. Please don't make me give you an order.'

Auntie Nags fluttered her hands in indignation, but then her photoreceptors went dark.

'What is it, Zare?' his mother asked in a small voice.

'Dhara didn't run away,' he said.

'I know that.'

'No – I mean, I can prove it.'

And then he told her about the farmers, and the status changes, and how he'd been accepted before anyone else. And about what he had decided to do.

'No, Zare,' his mother breathed. 'No, no, no. It's too dangerous.'

'It's the only way, Mim!'

'No, it isn't! Stop being crazy! I'm not losing you too, Zare!'

'You won't,' Zare said. 'The answers we need are in the Academy. They won't be able to take me by surprise, like they did Dhara. Unlike her, I'll have help. And if I get even a hint that they're coming for me, I really will run away. I promise you.'

His mother looked at him in astonishment, her eyes wide, her mouth hanging open. She closed her eyes for a long moment.

When she opened them again, her gaze was steely and determined.

'We can't tell your father,' she said.

Merei was right: Zare's refiled application was quickly accepted. When they got the news, Zare and his mother agreed that making things look right would require another party – though this would be a more somber affair, with a smaller guest list.

The preparations went smoothly, with Auntie Nags discreetly not mentioning that she'd been so rudely shut down, though her photoreceptors briefly flared red whenever she looked at Zare or his mother. The only snag came a couple of hours before the guests arrived, when Tepha discovered they were out of jogan-fruit.

'It's been in short supply all summer,' she said. 'Could you run down to the marketplace, Zare?'

Zare searched through the warren of stalls and stands, trying not to let his gaze linger on the white towers of the Academy looming over the marketplace. It took him nearly fifteen minutes to find any jogan, and the price was ridiculously high. He handed his credits to the vendor, only to find the man looking over Zare's shoulder, brows etched with concern.

Zare turned and watched a troop transport glide to a halt in the middle of the marketplace. It settled with a sigh of repulsorlifts and an Imperial officer disembarked, followed by a squad of stormtroopers.

They began striding towards Zare.

He knew there was nowhere to run and simply waited.

The stormtroopers scanned the line of stalls, with one trooper's armoured mask seeming to linger on Zare's face. Then they hurried past him, heading for a shuttered shop. As shoppers and merchants watched, the troopers levered open the door.

'DX-578! Remember your search procedure!' the officer yelled.

A minute later the troopers emerged with three men whose hands were bound behind their backs. The third was Beck.

The stormtroopers marched their prisoners past Zare, close enough that he could have touched them.

Beck's eyes jumped to Zare, and he offered him a

flicker of a smile. Zare looked at the armoured faces of each of the troopers as they passed. They were all alike. The troops led Beck and his two companions to the rear of the troop transport, then shoved them inside as the hustle and babble of the market resumed.

'Kid!' the vendor barked, yanking irritably on Zare's sleeve. 'You forgot your jogan-fruit!'

It was a beautiful evening on Lothal. Through his bedroom window Zare could smell seedpods and blossoms in the air.

Auntie Nags stopped fussing with his tunic, inspected him, and declared him ready for viewing. He looked at himself in the mirror and found a perfect young Imperial looking back.

And that's what I will be, he promised his reflection. *I will enter the Academy, say the right things, and succeed. I will learn how the Empire works. I will find Dhara. And I will wait for the resistance to develop, for someone to rebel.*

And then I will help those rebels bring the Empire down.

He nodded and walked up to the top deck, shaking hands with ministers and bureaucrats and neighbours. Commandant Aresko and Grint arrived and began monopolising the trays of dainties that Auntie Nags brought around. Merei hugged him, her smile faltering slightly. Standing by the railing, Lieutenant Roddance nodded at him, and Zare forced himself to look the young officer in the eye and nod back.

And then Governor Pryce and her attendants were there, making their way through the guests to where Zare waited with Merei. His father stood on one side of them, sombre but proud. His mother stood on the other, her thoughts her own.

The governor's aide hushed the crowd and she spoke briefly. She saluted the Leonises for their dedication to the Empire, and promised that the search for Dhara was not over. And then she turned to Zare.

'Congratulations on your appointment to the Academy,' she said. 'We're all honoured by your example, Zare. And I'm looking forward to finding out how you'll be of service to the galaxy.'

Zare shook the governor's hand and smiled.

'I'm looking forward to that, too,' he said.